Return to Hendre Ddu

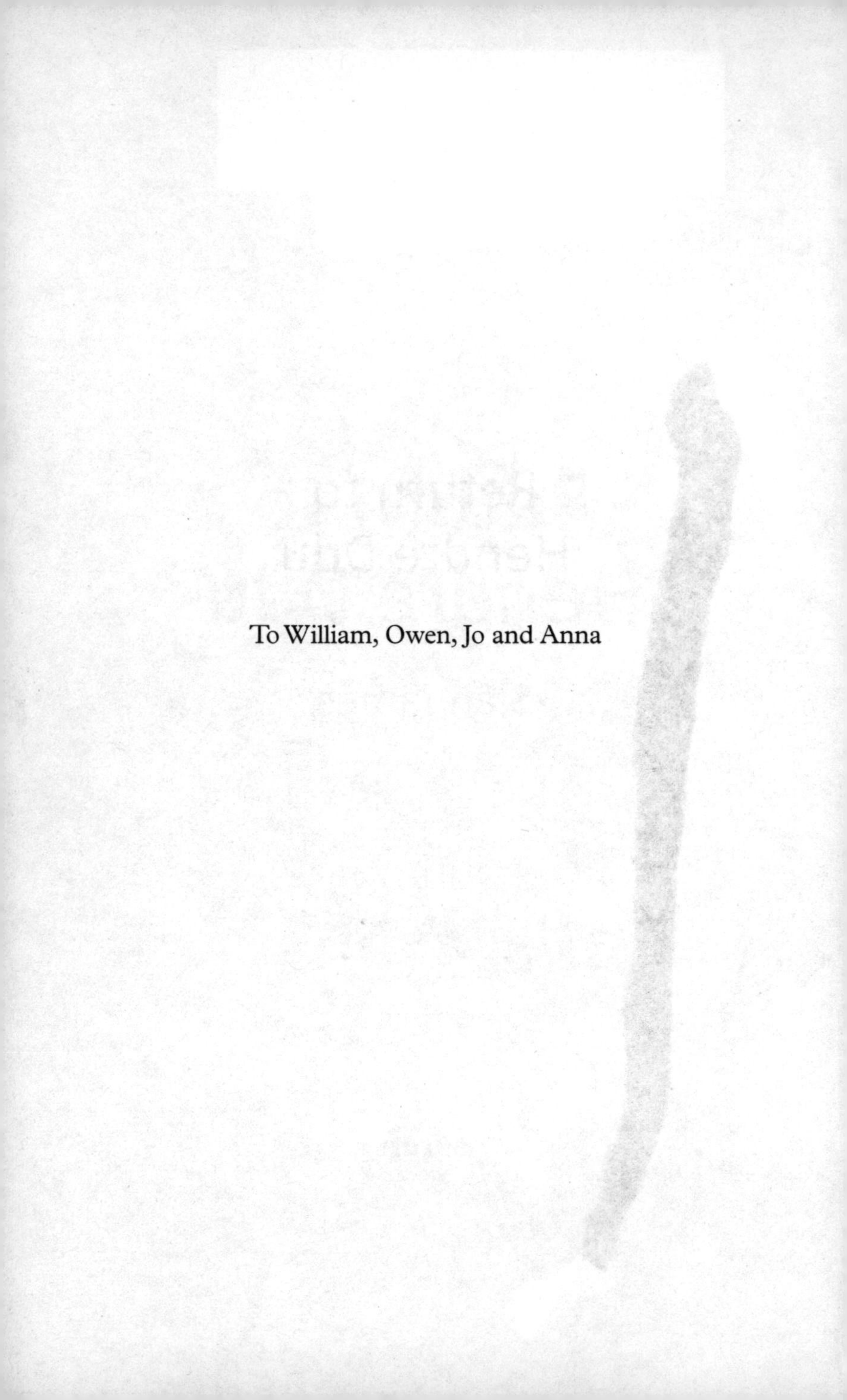

To William, Owen, Jo and Anna

Return to Hendre Ddu

Siân James

seren

seren is the book imprint of Poetry Wales Press Ltd
57 Nolton Street, Bridgend, Wales CF31 3AE
www.seren-books.com

ISBN 978-1-85411-488-4

A CIP record for this title is available from the British Library.

Printed in Plantin by Bell and Bain, Glasgow

The publisher acknowledges the financial support of the Welsh Books Council.

Return to Hendre Ddu

Chapter one

'And where is Mari Elen today?' were Nano's first words as Lowri turned up at Hendre Ddu one warm June afternoon. 'Come and sit down, for goodness sake. You're looking quite pale.'

'She's out with Mr Ifans, I mean, out with Josi,' Lowri said. 'He's taken her out on horseback. She loves being with her father.'

'No harm in that. And it gives you a bit of peace and quiet, no doubt. She's a lively child, I know that.'

'But I do get lonely, Miss Rees.'

'Yes, and something else as well, child, to judge by your face. Marriage is not proving so easy, perhaps.'

'It's easy enough. I mean the work is easy enough. I'm through with the chickens and the baking and the cleaning by ten o'clock every morning.'

'You were always a good little worker. I had no fears that you'd find it too much for you and I knew that Mr Ifans wouldn't be a demanding husband, but you miss us because this was your family and everyone misses their family when they get married. Now don't cry. A good talk and two fresh eggs for your tea and you'll feel much better. You are still very young, Lowri, and there's no one to keep an eye on you up in Cefn Hebog. Never mind; marriage isn't easy, but you'll get used to it. You haven't been used to an idle life and you're not the sort of girl to have foolish expectations. Oh I've had girls, good girls too, leaving me to get married and they think that life is going to be all laughter and loving and it's those who have a shock. Especially if they marry a widower with several children and never an empty moment. It's then that they miss Miss Rees who always kept an eye on them to see that they weren't doing too much. You remember those afternoons when I used to send you out to pick blackberries or blackcurrants in the orchard? I only wanted you to have a change and a rest and a bit of good fresh air. I never asked or wanted anyone to work too hard.'

'You were always very good to me, Miss Rees.'

'Of course I was, because you were a good girl. Now that Ceridwen Morris who was here a few years before you, I had to get rid of her and it's not an easy thing to do. A girl without a good reference often finds it very difficult to get another job in a decent house. But I explained to Mrs Ifans, God rest her soul, that it was necessary. I have a family here, I said, all the girls are treated as family and they're never kept away from Miss Catrin and Mister Tom so I have to be specially careful that no one has any corrupting influence on them.'

She understood at once. 'Thank you, Nano,' she said, 'for your care.'

'You and Miss Catrin were good friends and I had not a moment's anxiety on that score. As Mister Tom wrote to me when he heard that you were going to marry his father: "Lowri is a lovely girl, she will make my father a good wife and she will be a kind and loving mother to Mari Elen." Catrin was equally happy. You see, we all had every faith and confidence in you. I know without you telling me what your present trouble is and I want to assure you that it will pass. Mr Ifans has been dealt a double blow, the wife he loved and the woman who led him astray both dying within ten days of one another. Of course he was left reeling with shock. For a time, as you know, he lived alone and friendless and when he turned up here on that March day he looked and smelt like a tramp: well you saw him, you were here with me and it was you had to burn all his clothes at the bottom of the orchard if I remember right. Now he is trying to come to terms with his great loss and he will turn to you eventually. He knows your worth, you must be patient. His wife was a saint, it's not easy to live up to a saint, and the other was a sinner.

'No, don't look at me like that Lowri, we must face facts: a woman who entices a man away from his legal wife is not a good woman, a witch she might have been called in the old days. I remember in school we learned about that witch Anne Boleyn who had enticed some fat old king away from his true religious wife. There are such women. You are neither a saint nor a sinner but an ordinary, good, hard-working woman, and in time he will turn to you. You must be patient. Before too long you will have a little baby of your own and with a new family, Mr Ifans will become a new man, I promise you. Miss Catrin, who'll have her baby soon, is very happy. You must visit her; these things seem to be catching quite often. So Mr Ifans rides out with only Mari Elen as company, I've heard about that. Ianto saw them in the Sheaf the other day where she was attracting a lot of attention sitting there with her father like a little princess and demanding this and that. He never spoilt Tom and Catrin that way. But it won't do her much harm, perhaps. You could say I'd asked to see her, then you might be able to bring her here for a few days which could bring her down to earth a bit. Catrin was a proper little madam when she was two or three and poor Mrs Ifans was very worried about her. Of course Mari Elen will be able to start school now that she's three. That will do her a lot of good. Little ones don't have to attend in the afternoon, but I think Mari Elen will want to. She'll be fascinated by all the other children, she's a gregarious little thing and she'll love all the learning too. Anyone can see how bright she is. Her half-sister Catrin was exactly the same.

'Now then, I'm going to give you the same good tea that I give the Reverend Isaacs when he calls and he always looks better when he rides away. No, marriage isn't easy, I know that, but it's worth your best efforts, dear Lowri.'

Being called dear Lowri and being treated like a visitor was too much. Lowri burst into tears but Nano, busying herself with boiling a couple of fresh eggs and buttering some still warm scones, appeared not to notice.

When she left to walk up the long hill to Cefn Hebog,

Lowri realised that she hadn't had to relate any of her troubles to Miss Rees. She seemed to have known about them all and only advised her to be patient. Mr Ifans, Josi rather, would turn to her eventually if only she was patient and loving. She would be patient and loving, of course she would, but it was the nights which were the worst, the nights were often very long. She went to bed feeling tired but after about ten minutes she was wide awake and wondering where he was. He often went out for long, dark walks and then slept in the little attic bedroom which was both cold and damp. He said he wasn't going to sleep with her while he was so restless. 'No use us both being awake all night, Lowri,' he'd said, though she would have welcomed being awake with him. Her body cried out for his closeness and warmth. Was Miss Rees right? Would he turn to her, his ordinary little wife, if she was patient and loving? She had to believe it. She simply had to.

Mari Elen and her father were back at the cottage by the time she returned from the farm.

'Where were you?' Mari Elen shouted out, running towards her peevishly.

'We wondered where you'd got to, cariad,' Josi explained. 'We were both worried that you'd run away from us.'

'Don't ever go away again,' Mari Elen demanded. 'I want you to be here when I get home. I don't want you to go out without us. Where have you been?'

'I went to Hendre Ddu to talk to Miss Rees and she insisted that I stayed to tea,' Lowri explained.

'You stayed to tea without me,' Mari Elen complained,

'that wasn't kind. That wasn't kind, was it Dada?'

'Well, you go out without Lowri, don't you, bach?'

'Yes, but I always want her to come with us. Only she's always got work to do. Washing the floor, feeding those nasty old hens and searching for eggs.'

'We must wait and take her with us tomorrow. Tell her what a lovely dinner we have in the Sheaf.'

'I prefer dinner at home. I like the dinner that Lowri cooks best. Especially her liver and bacon and especially her apple tart.'

'We'll stay home tomorrow little one, and in the afternoon I'll take you both out to Hendre Ddu in the pony and trap.'

'Good. I don't like going out without my little mother.'

It was the first time Mari Elen had ever called Lowri her little mother. Lowri's eyes filled with tears. She felt suddenly happy. She felt that Miss Rees might be right after all.

'Do you miss Hendre Ddu, little one?' Josi asked her that night after Mari Elen had been put to bed.

'I do, in a way. Miss Rees was hard on all of us, none of us was allowed to be idle for even five minutes, but she took good care of us as well and never made us work too hard. I remember I never had to tell her when I was ill or in pain, she knew by my pale face, and she'd find some easy tasks for me. We were her family and she was very kind to us in her own way. She told me how she'd hated having to dismiss Ceridwen Morris that time. I wonder what Ceridwen had done to offend her?'

'I think I could tell you, but I'd rather not. It doesn't reflect well on me.'

'Oh, I see. You were flirting with her, you dreadful man.'

'I suppose so. Anyway, Miriam put a stop to all that. I never flirted with anyone after meeting Miriam.'

'And Miss Rees thinks she was a sinner.'

'You don't though, do you, my love?'

'No. I saw you together once and realised how it was with you.'

'You're very wise and very tender and you'll be my saviour yet, but not quite yet. I haven't forgiven myself yet. I haven't yet made my peace with Rachel or with Miriam.'

'I think they've both forgiven you. Now you have to try to forgive yourself.'

'I try. I do try.'

Lowri was happier in bed that night, though she was still on her own.

When they arrived at Hendre Ddu the next afternoon, they found the place in uproar. A letter had arrived from Tom telling them he had been wounded and was to be invalided out of the army. He was due home within the week. Miss Rees' words tumbled out of her. 'Steady now, Nano, gan bwyll,' Josi said. 'Where's the letter you had?'

'Wounded, wounded. How badly it doesn't tell us, but it must be pretty serious or they wouldn't be sending him home, would they? They have these field hospitals that Catrin was telling us about for soldiers that are only slightly wounded. I've told Dr Andrews that he must be here as soon as I get word that Tom has landed in England. Dr Andrews is a wonderful doctor as we all know and now he's family as well, Catrin having a bit of sense at last. And you, Mr Ifans, must stay here with us from now on. We've had enough of your grieving by this time. Life goes on. There is a time for mourning and a time to refrain from mourning as it tells us in the good book. What is your son going to think of a father who can't look after his farm while he's fighting abroad? Lowri, you and Mari Elen must come back here tonight so that I have an extra pair of hands for all the nursing I'll be called upon to do. Sali was only a child and I had to send her back home as you know. She's got a job cleaning at the vicarage now, and being home with her parents at night will suit her better. I'm glad she won't be here when Mister Tom comes home because she'd bother him. She told him once that she wasn't happy here and he asked me what we could do about it. Quite worked up about it he was. Well, how could she be happy here when her good mistress had just died and her sister was leaving to get married. But that bit of notice from Mister Tom went to her head and she started telling people that he had promised her this, that and the other, so I had to ask your mother to take her away. Your mother quite understood. Sali had always been one for romanticising, she said, and I couldn't be doing with that. How would Mister Tom feel if he found out that the girl had been inventing all sorts of lies about him and had been spreading those lies among anyone who'd listen? Now, you and Mr Ifans can have the front bedroom with Mari Elen in the small dressing room, it'll be big enough for her little bed. Now, what else have I got to think about? Lowri, don't stand about any more, girl, get an apron on and then I'll be able to treat you as an equal again. There's meals to prepare and Tom's bedroom to get ready. What will you do? I'll get Maudie to help you. She's a good girl, but she needs someone to keep an eye on her. Mr Ifans, go out on the clos and ask old Prosser what you can do to help. He's complaining day and night that he has too much to do. Don't stand about, man. Your son is coming home wounded and he won't want to find everything here at sixes and sevens. Do as I tell you now, Mr Ifans. You've got a good heart, I've always known that. Now, Mari Elen, no more nonsense about wanting your Dada every moment. Your big brother, Tom, is coming home and I'll be wanting your Dada to look after him. You'll have to play on your own or I'll be tying you into that little chair in that corner, just as I used to do to your half-sister, Catrin, when she was a little girl. I haven't got time to look after naughty children and neither has Lowri.'

'I don't like you very much Miss Rees,' Mari Elen told her in a hurt but very reasonable voice.

'I suppose I'll have to live with that for the time being,' Nano told her. 'We're all too busy now to play. Mister Tom is coming home.'

Later that evening Catrin arrived on the farm holding herself like a queen, proudly pregnant. Her father kissed her and Nano relaxed for a moment and told her how well she was looking. 'I like these honeymoon babies,' she told them all. 'It shows that the parents mean business. It's time for you, Mr Ifans, to think about a little sister or brother for that little Miss over there, who's becoming far too spoilt.'

'No, she's not, Nano. She's perfect and I don't want her different. You never complained that Tom and Catrin were spoilt.'

'I wonder if Tom is still hearing from that retired colonel's daughter, May something? Your poor mother was very pleased that he had a nice young lady promising to write to him. A lot can happen in a letter, can't it Mr Ifans? Oh, I remember how my dear Rachel used to hang about for the postman when you were first courting. That was a happy time, though her father was hopping mad, do you remember? He'd wanted her to marry that ugly old fellow, Jim Reynolds, Dôl Goch. But he was too old for her anyway. I was glad you'd turned up, though I know I gave you a hard time at the beginning.'

Chapter two

'I wish we were back at Cefn Hebog,' Lowri said when Josi joined her in bed that night. 'I don't feel right here in Mrs Ifans' bed.'

'Neither do I, but we'll soon get used to it. Come and cwtch here with me. I had to stay, you know. I've neglected the lad's farm for too long. I'll have to try to whip it into shape now, the hedges are in a dreadful state. It's I who should set them to rights because I learnt the art of hedging from my father. You cut about three-quarters of the way through a branch, near the base, so that new growth will shoot out from it in the spring, with a hazel or an ash sapling hammered in every few yards to strengthen it. Yes, my father, Jasper Evans, was a master hedger and he taught me the way of it. But I haven't the time this year, it's a labour-intensive task and I'll have to look to the cattle and the horses and leave the hedging to the others for this year. I don't want Tom to think the farm's been neglected, though I know it has; poor Prosser has done all he can. And poor Miss Rees has had to work too hard for years now.

She must be well into her seventies you know, and should be taking it easy. You'll be such a help to her. She won't make you work too hard, either, because she'll know I'll be looking out for you. And I suppose it's true that Mari Elen is getting too much of her own way with you and me. Neither of us seems to be a match for her, but Nano has some natural authority. Tom and Catrin always behaved well when she was in charge. Poor Tom. How will we find him, I wonder. Did you know about little Sali losing her heart to him?'

'No. I was told they'd taken her away because she was lonely and unhappy here. She's always been a foolish little creature, but I half understand how Tom's feelings must have affected her. He was so sad about his mother and about leaving Hendre Ddu that she must have felt that some of it was about leaving her. Girls can be very foolish creatures if they have no one to bring them down to earth. If I'd known how she felt I would have been able to put her right. For instance, I would have told her about this sweetheart of his, I'm sure that would have altered her feelings.'

'Nano mentioned this sweetheart. Of course, I'd been told nothing about her.'

'I think Miss Rees made a great deal out of hearing that some nice girl or other, a retired colonel's daughter if I remember rightly, had promised to write to him. It was to raise poor Mrs Ifans' spirits when she was so loath to let him go abroad.'

'I was loath to let him go abroad, too. And I told him so

more than once. I thought he was mad to enlist. I only hope he isn't too badly injured.'

The next morning a War Office letter arrived letting them know that Tom had lost his right leg at the knee and was to be invalided out of the army; an honourable discharge they called it. He'd been in the field hospital for more than a month and he was doing very well.

Nano fainted on hearing the news but Lowri and Josi soon realised that this was no ordinary faint, she had suffered a stroke and had to be carried to her bed which proved no easy task, even for Josi and Davy Prosser between them. Dr Andrews and Catrin were called and Nano insisted that they, too, were to stay for the foreseeable future.

Catrin and Lowri hugged each other, both terrified by what had happened. Nano had always seemed indestructible; Hendre Ddu without her at the helm was unimaginable. They sat at her side, stroking her stricken face, talking to her and listening to her heavy breathing.

'Tell us the truth,' Josi begged his son-in-law when they were back downstairs. 'Is there any hope of a recovery? Any hope at all?'

'She's strong and healthy and her heart is sound so she'll get a little better quite soon. She'll soon be sitting up and trying to talk, but a complete recovery is unlikely I'm afraid. She's suffered a major stroke. Let's hope that Tom's arrival helps her recover. She dotes on him, I believe.'

'She dotes on him, of course she does, and on Catrin too. And she's eagerly looking forward to the baby's arrival, I know that. She's got a lot to live for.'

Catrin and Lowri made up the bed in the guest room for Catrin and her husband. 'You should have our bed, by rights,' Lowri told Catrin when they'd finished.

'What rights are those then?' Catrin asked. 'My father is the head of the house, at least until Tom arrives home and you are his legal wife so doesn't that give you a right to the best bedroom? Stop putting yourself down. When you came to be a maid here, my mother told Tom and me that you were our cousin and that we were to treat you as family and I'm sure we always did. Now why can't you accept that, since we always have. You're now my step-mother and I'll respect your judgement and try to agree with everything you suggest.'

'Don't be silly,' was Lowri's only response. 'And don't let Nano hear you saying things like that. She doesn't hold with all this equality. Oh, Catrin, what will we do if she dies?'

'She's going to get better. Perhaps she'll never be really well again but she's going to make a partial recovery, Graham seems quite confident of that. She'll always be in charge, will always be able to tell us what to do. We have to believe that.'

'Where is Nano?' Mari Elen asked as she came in from the yard for tea.

'She's not well so she's having an afternoon in bed,' Josi told her.

'Take her some hot milk and two Marie biscuits,' was Mari Elen's suggestion. 'That will put colour in her cheeks. I don't much like her but I don't like her being ill. When I'm ill Lowri puts her cold hand on my forehead and it makes me feel much better.'

'We'll have to hire a full-time nurse,' Dr Andrews said. 'I believe that Nurse Griffin, Nyth Brain, is a large, capable woman.'

'Oh no,' Lowri moaned. 'Miss Rees hates Mrs Griffin, Nyth Brain. She frightened poor Mrs Ifans terribly one day, mentioning that word 'cancer' to her when no one else had dared mention it. Miss Rees almost attacked her on the spot and she's never spoken to her since. She won't even go to any chapel social or village eisteddfod now for fear that Mrs Griffin will be there. I'd rather do all the nursing myself than leave her to that woman.'

'You're far too small and delicate,' Dr Andrews said. 'Miss Rees will have to be lifted and turned two or three times a day and she's a fair weight. All the same I'm glad you told me about the animosity between her and Nurse Griffin, that would never do. I'll have to find someone else in Cardigan. I know the deputy matron of the women's hospital there and she's sure to be able to suggest someone suitable, someone she's trained. And perhaps I ought to go now, there's no time to lose.'

'What about your dinner?' Catrin asked, but he'd already disappeared.

They had to have their meal without him, but Catrin assured them that it was perfectly normal for her husband to miss at least one meal every day.

'Well, doctors don't do too much hard manual work, do they? Their work is very important, I know that, but it's not hot sweaty work like men on the farm do. Or take the horses, now. Nobody would ask a good working mare to miss her meal. It's like the petrol for a car, you've got to keep them going.'

'I have to miss supper very often when Lowri puts me to bed early. And I'm busy all day long.'

Their chatter floated over Lowri's head, she was far too worried to listen.

At least Graham's errand proved worthwhile. The deputy matron had been able to recommend a competent and conscientious nurse who had recently finished her previous job and could start the following morning. 'Another bed to be made up,' Catrin grumbled, 'all the same it will be good to have an extra pair of hands.'

'I don't think she'll be prepared to do any housework,' Graham warned.

'No, I've noticed that it's only wives who have to turn their hands to anything and everything.'

When Tom arrived home the next day, he managed, with the help of one of his crutches and some gentle pushing from his father, to negotiate the stairs to see Nano and when he spoke to her, she regained consciousness and smiled at him. Everyone felt jubilant though it was only a small step forward.

'This will do me a lot of good,' Tom said later. 'I'm not the invalid now, and I'm feeling much better for it. I was feeling very sorry for myself, coming home like this, but now I realise that there are much more important things. I'm out of the hell of France, I'm thankful to be alive and happy to be home. I'm going to be all right. You shall see.'

Catrin kissed him and Lowri fetched him some tiny new potatoes with butter and buttermilk, which had always been his favourite snack.

'You've lost a leg, I hear,' Mari Elen said, like one struggling to make polite conversation. 'Can I look up your trouser leg?'

'You may. But I'm afraid there isn't much to see except for bandages. You may like to see it when the district nurse comes to change the dressings.'

'I would, thank you. I think I'm going to like you though you're a bit old for a brother. I'd prefer a baby brother but all the same I like your face.'

'And I like yours. I hope we'll be great friends. Shall we shake hands? Or kiss, perhaps?'

'Not at the moment. I don't know you well enough yet. But in a day or two I may like to kiss you.'

'I look forward to that.'

'My goodness, she's a bright little thing,' Tom said later that evening when she'd been carried off to bed. 'I thought of her as a baby still.'

'She was three a few months ago, a schoolgirl now, and already quite a character in the area. You and I will soon be known as her brother and sister I've no doubt.'

'And when is your baby due? I only have to turn my back on you for five minutes and this is what happens. Mother would have been thrilled though, wouldn't she, to be a mamgu. I can see her so vividly as she was when I first remember her, a regal figure in a splendid cream high-necked dress with lace frills on the bosom, women had such important bosoms in those days – what's happened to them – and her gold watch on a long gold chain. Do you know Catrin, I really felt her presence at my side when I was first wounded and hovering between life and death. Don't mention it to anyone, or they'll think I'm touched in the head. All the same, I felt she was near me, I really did.'

'Tom dear, I wish we'd been closer as children. We were always quarrelling weren't we? Perhaps we'll find ways of being close now. I feel it was you who brought me the greatest joy of my life, my love for Edward. Even now that he's been dead for over three years, I still feel his love surrounding me. Perhaps it's not so far from the way you feel about mother's presence.'

'The living and the dead are very close, I've realised that. While I was in hospital, hot and sweaty with very little pain relief, I used to go over and over the Reverend Isaacs' sermons. Yet at the time, I hardly knew I was listening to them. He was a great pacifist of course, and I wish I'd paid more attention to his words. I found nothing worth fighting for, the glory of war is a fabrication: there is no glory. There certainly is sacrifice and unbelievable bravery amongst the common soldiers but the high-ranking officers send men over the top every morning with absolutely no pity. Up those scaling ladders and they're shot as soon as their heads appear over the parapet. I wouldn't send a horse into those battlefields and they are ready to send hundreds of young men to their almost certain death. Of course it was my duty to blow the whistle, but it was always, always against my better judgement. I do hope no one ever tells me that I was wounded in a great cause or I shall refute it. I lost my leg in a stupid battle for a few hundred yards of territory of no earthly use to anyone.

'Some of those poor Welsh and Welsh-speaking country lads I met out there were totally bewildered and shell-shocked and yet if they turned their back on the heavy bombardment in front of them they were shot as traitors. I'm ashamed of volunteering for active service. I wouldn't feel so badly about it if I'd been conscripted as men are now. But no, I went out of some feeling of comradeship I suppose, with all those other fools who were enlisting. I was never a true patriot like Edward. Well, I only hope he was killed before finding out what a sham it all was, all for material gain, and how useless his sacrifice was. Don't tell Father how I feel, he'd despise me more than ever.'

'He doesn't despise you. I saw him in tears the night you left for France though I never saw him break down for Mother's death or Miriam's. He's had a lot to deal with, poor man, but I think he's achieved some sort of peace now with dear Lowri. What a treasure she is, though she still refers to him as Mr Ifans and I am often Miss Catrin however many times I correct her. Christ promised that the meek should inherit the earth, didn't he, though she's only inherited Father and that little madam, Mari Elen. I was cruel to her mother, Tom, did you ever hear about that? Yes, I met Miriam once in the chemist's in town and I followed her out and gave her such a mouthful. It's an episode that still grieves me, though I suppose she had much worse to put up with, even her aunt turned against her, I heard. And yet she was once a highly respected school teacher. Her funeral was a very quiet almost secret affair of course, but the very first village meeting afterwards was really all about her, one person after another wanting to tell everyone how much she did for them; her pupils thought the world of her. Teachers in our elementary schools are usually not much brighter than the pupils they try to teach, but she was very highly regarded. And she is still talked about, so Teifi Griffiths, a former pupil who became a journalist on *The Tivyside*, said in her obituary. She certainly wasn't an ordinary woman and I misjudged her.'

'Of course you did. You were only conscious that she had broken up our family. I felt quite as strongly about it as you did.'

'And at that time, I knew nothing of the power of love.... Well, aren't we having an elevated conversation? Let me bring it down to earth and ask you whether you have a sweetheart. Miss Rees seems to think you have. I must confess I knew nothing of it, which shows how very distant we always were.'

'I still cherish the memory of a very charming girl I met before I was sent abroad. But I only mentioned her to Nano because she seemed to need something to think about in those dark days when Mother was dying. I hear from her from time to time, and perhaps a bit oftener, but I won't expect to hear from her again after I tell her my news.'

'Tom! What a very poor opinion you have of women. I would have gladly given my life to looking after a wounded Edward if only I'd had that chance. Anyway, you must invite her to visit us here. She may be very glad of a few peaceful days in the country and some good country fare. Things are terrible in London, it seems. I look forward to meeting her. Though Nano may not be with us to toil and cook for quite some time, Lowri and I will do our best to make her feel at home. We've both been trained by Nano, you know, so I'm sure we'll manage excellently between us. And Lowri says Maud and Lottie are good girls too. What do you say?'

'I'm not sure. I don't think things have gone as far as that. But I'll think about it.'

'And don't take too long about it or someone else will get there before you. Oh, I can hear Graham's motor car in the yard now. I wonder why he's so late?'

Catrin went out to the porch to meet her husband.

In the quiet days that followed, Catrin heavy with child, she and Tom found a friendship that had always been denied to them as children.

'I was always jealous of you,' Tom confessed. 'You were Father's favourite and I couldn't put up with that. I knew I was Mother's favourite but that never meant so much to me. I worshipped Father and could hardly bear it when he left us. It's only now that I can see him as an ordinary man with the usual human frailties. It's a strange thing Catrin, but I had to go to France before really appreciating my own family and my own country. I love Wales. Not only her peaceful beauty but all her ordinary, poor people. I mean, Davy Prosser, for instance, who works every day, sometimes until very late at night out of some feeling of loyalty to our family. What have we ever done to deserve such loyalty? We pay him a pittance, the amount a senior farm labourer is always paid, I suppose, and he seems ready to give us his entire life in return. Can you imagine Prosser being spiteful or mean to any one of us? No, he always gives us his best and I intend to put his wages up in the autumn and every autumn from now on. I'm determined to make the farm pay, not to make money for myself for improvements to the house and land and so on, but so that I can be a decent employer, trying to pay back the men for their labour. I want to wipe out the memory of Mother's grandfather, old Thomas Morgan, who cheated and stole from the little men, lending them money and snaffling their smallholdings when they couldn't repay the loans. Pray God, I have none of his blood in me. How I wish I were able-bodied so that I could get up at six every morning and get started on the work. But there, if I were fit I'd still be in that hell hole in France among the rats and the rotting corpses.

'And now,' he continued, 'I must get myself up those dratted stairs that seem to be so much steeper than they used to be, to sit with Nano for a while. She's not very cheerful, I'm afraid. She realises now that she's had a stroke and keeps begging me to shoot her. But I tell her that Dr Andrews assures me I can still get some work out of her sooner or later, so I'm giving her a few weeks to recover.

I've never been into her bedroom before. It was always forbidden territory, wasn't it? She has every picture we ever painted on her walls and all the poems we used to be persuaded to write her for Christmas every year, all highly embarrassing. She does look better today though, her face isn't as lop-sided as it was. I wish that letter from the war office hadn't given her such a fright, 'wounded' would have been quite bad enough.'

'I'll come up with you,' Catrin said. 'Then she can tell me once again how to prepare for my labour. She wants me to drink raspberry leaf tea every morning and to eat hard-boiled eggs for at least one meal every day. It's something those famous physicans of Myddfai used to recommend in the last century. She's told me already that I'm carrying a lusty boy who'll weigh ten pounds and look exactly like you.'

'But with two legs, I hope,' Tom said as they went slowly upstairs.

They found that Nano wasn't fond of her new nurse, though she conceded that she wasn't as rough as Mrs Griffin. 'But she grunts and snores all night,' she told them. 'How is that helping to cure me? What wages are you proposing to give her? She eats like a horse and wipes her mouth on my clean towels. I can't wait to dismiss her.'

'You shall dismiss her as soon as you're able to sit up and eat a good meal. That shouldn't take you too long. You've always been strong.'

'How is Lowri managing in the kitchen? Tell her that Lottie is to prepare all the vegetables and do all the washing up. Don't let her spoil Lottie now that I've managed to train her. She is to clean out the range at six in the morning and scrub the kitchen floor and the dairy. It's only what Lowri herself had to do when she was fourteen and it didn't do her any harm. Lottie is slow but she knows her jobs, getting the eggs and churning the butter and laying the table for dinner when she's changed her dress.'

She stopped talking for a while and lay breathing heavily, but was soon ready to start again. Her words were not as rushed as usual and her speech was a little slurred. 'Don't let her become slovenly; she's got to be watched, has Lottie. And remember Mrs Ifans, God rest her soul, couldn't put up with a slovenly servant waiting at table. "Get her to wash her face and pin up her hair, Nano," she'd tell me. "Buy her some scented soap and a good strong comb and compliment her when she's made an effort." I always did. "And see that she mends any tear in her dress and buys good quality stockings even if they cost a few pennies more. Give her an extra sixpence when she buys something useful instead of spending her wages on rubbish from the tinker." '

Another pause, longer this time, while she gathered what strength she could still muster. '"Teach her your ways, Nano," she used to say, God bless her sweet soul. Maudie is more dependable, being a bit older. You can go down now, you two. There's no need for you to spend any more time with a stupid old woman who should have had the decency to make a tidy job of dying instead of landing up like this, a useless weight on the bed and costing good money to feed and nurse.'

An even longer pause, but when Catrin tried to make an excuse for leaving, she refused to let go her hand. 'Remember, both of you, I've got my best linen nightdress wrapped up in that top drawer for a shroud and I'm leaving all my good dresses and my shoes to my cousin Mary Ann Hopkins in Tregaron, my real pearl necklace to you, Miss Catrin, and my sapphire brooch with seed pearls to Mister Tom's wife and my three or four books to Mrs Prosser who's a bit of a bookworm as I was whenever I got the time, which I never did. Go down now please. You're tiring me with all this chatter.'

'Wouldn't it be dreadful if Lottie or Maudie left now that they haven't got Nano to keep an eye on them and order them about. Do you think an extra sixpence a week would keep them happy Tom? What Father used to do was try to hire a really handsome young lad at Michaelmas for the young maids to fall in love with. We'll have to do that. Tom, let's be real friends from now on. You don't have to look after me now, do you? I'm a respectable married woman. You used to be so bossy, so frightened that I'd turn out badly.'

'I'm sure I was. And I needn't have feared, you didn't turn out too badly.'

Mari Elen had bought some humbugs for Nano and her father said she could take them upstairs to her but that she must be down in five minutes.

She made the most of her time. 'Miss Rees,' she said. 'I'm afraid your face has slipped down on one side.'

'Yes, I'm afraid it has,' Miss Rees agreed, rather glumly.

'My father thought it best not to tell you, but I think it would be unkind to let you have a shock when you saw yourself in a mirror.'

'I see what you mean.'

'In any case, you're not young and beautiful like Catrin, for instance. It would be much worse, I think, if her face had collapsed. Perhaps Graham would no longer want to be married to her.'

'Oh, I hope he would. When you get married you promise to love someone in sickness and in health.'

'I don't think I shall get married. I think I'll choose to stay with my father and Lowri.'

'I think that would be a very wise move. They're good people and will never let you down.'

'Anyway I'll go now, Miss Rees. You won't worry about your poor face, will you? We'll all still love you. Or at least I know I will.'

'Thank you.'

'You must remind me to visit poor Miss Rees every day,' she told Lowri when she got downstairs, 'I think I cheer her up.'

'Well, perhaps you do,' Lowri said, but without too much conviction.

Chapter three

At about three o'clock the following morning when the farm was completely quiet at last, Tom had his first nightmare. His loud screams were terrifying, those of a man at the brink of some unimaginable disaster. Josi rushed in to his bedroom while Lowri stayed to comfort Mari Elen who had been woken by the noise. Catrin was also awake and heard Miss Rees' bell being rung.

'It's Mister Tom, poor soul,' she said as Catrin went in and lit a candle in her room.

'Great heavens, Nano you're sitting up in bed,' Catrin said. 'How wonderful. Graham said that you'd soon be back to normal.'

'Of course I'm sitting up in bed,' Miss Rees said. 'How could I remain on my back with no one attending to Mister Tom. Mr Ifans was so slow getting up. I rang the bell, though, because I can't seem to get myself down again. Could you give me a good heave, Catrin, please, or I'll be sitting here until the day of judgement.'

Catrin managed to lay the old woman down and

offered her a cup of tea. 'I would appreciate a cup of tea,' she said, 'if you can wait to hold the cup. I feel I've been to hell and back. What terrible memories came back to torment that precious boy who I held in my arms when he was barely five minutes old? Why wasn't someone sleeping at his side to protect him from those dreadful dreams? His father should be in there with him. I'll have to get a small bed into his room so that he's never left on his own again. Oh, why has the Good Lord decided to strike me down at this time when I could be of such service to the dear boy? Blessed be the name of our God, but there are certain things I'd like to take him to task about.'

'All the same, I don't think Tom would welcome anyone sleeping in his room to protect him. He's not a child, Nano.'

'Bring me a cup of tea, Catrin. I want to be fit by morning. Somehow I don't think you can manage without me.'

'I think we'll have to manage without you for the next few weeks, Nano. But you shall still tell us exactly what to do, I promise. You're still in charge.'

'A cup of tea first then and then a cup of tea for Mister Tom, and perhaps a beef sandwich. A beef sandwich with a touch of mustard gives a man great comfort somehow. Even a spot of medicinal brandy will do him no harm tonight.'

'I'll let him know what you say,' Catrin said.

'Mister Tom,' Miss Rees said a few days later, 'I don't think I've got long to live and if you saw how Dr Andrews looked at me this morning you'd have seen that he agreed with me.'

Tom was shaken. 'He doesn't know how tough you are,' he said at last, 'I often heard Mother tell us how ill you were when you had pneumonia, double pneumonia, that time. You weren't expected to live then, and that was many, many years ago.'

'I am a tough old bird, yes, and I may pull through, but again I may not. And, if not, I'd like to meet that May Malcolm you once told me about before I die. There was something in your voice when you mentioned her and I'd heard that very note once before when my dear Rachel first met your father. You said that she'd written to you very faithfully and that means a lot to me. I want to meet her, Tom. I want to tell her about your dear mother as well as many stories about your early life. Will you write to her this very afternoon and tell her that it's a matter of some urgency? When the call comes, Tom, a soul has to answer it, not plead for another few days. When she sees me, she'll understand that there was no time to lose.'

'I'll write to her this afternoon,' Tom promised, 'though she'll be very surprised by my letter I'm sure. I don't suppose she'll think I've ever mentioned her to anyone.'

'I don't know about that. When a person realises that something important has happened to them, they usually like to mention it. I'd be surprised if she hasn't mentioned you to her mother and father.'

'She has no mother, Nano. Her mother died when she was very young, sixteen I think. And I don't think you'll consider her very pretty, either. She's certainly not beautiful like Catrin. And she's a bit older than I am too.'

'Poor motherless child,' Miss Rees said and shut her eyes so that Tom felt he was dismissed.

'I feel very embarrassed,' Tom told Catrin and Lowri later that morning. 'Miss Rees insists that she's dying and that her dying wish is to meet May Malcolm who I'd mentioned to her on my embarkation leave years ago – how many years, it seems like a lifetime. What is the poor girl going to think?'

'She's going to think that you'd like to see her, and what's wrong with that? Send her a timetable of trains from London and say your brother-in-law will meet her at any time. Lowri will make one of her famous raspberry tarts and I'll cook some ham ready for supper. Good old Nano, I say.'

'What do you feel for this girl, Tom?' Josi asked later when he'd heard of Nano's demand. 'Is she an ordinary nice girl or is she special?'

'I'm not too sure, Father. She made a big impression on me and I certainly haven't forgotten her.'

'You'll know when you meet her again,' Catrin told him. 'You're older now and far more mature. I trust your judgement, somehow. Don't be nervous. You want to see her again and your family is humouring you. That's all she need think.'

'She'll think more than that,' Josi said. 'But then, what's the harm.'

Mari Elen was excited at the prospect of the new lady friend who couldn't speak Welsh.

'It's a good thing I've learnt some English,' she said.

'She'd be very upset if I couldn't talk to her. Poor Miss Rees doesn't have much English but I'll be able to help her. Isn't it a good thing that I'm here. How long are we staying, Lowri? I miss my little kitten, Ifor, and my pet duck but I know it's best I stay here for a while if only to practise my English with Miss May Malcolm.'

It was decided that it was Catrin who should write to Miss Malcolm giving her the news of Tom's injury – he hadn't yet told her – and explaining about their old nurse's stroke and her desire to see Mr Tom's young lady before she died.

> *Tom told her about you when he was on embarkation leave because our mother was then dying and he wanted to leave her and Miss Rees with some comforting news before he left. He has impressed upon me that there is nothing between you except that you promised to write to him, that you kept your promise and that he always looked forward to hearing from you. He is going through a very hard time at the moment as his leg had to be amputated at the knee. Knowing my brother as I do, I know it will not be long before he is on horseback again and my husband is also trying to persuade him to buy a motor car. All the same we all feel that it would do him a great deal of good to see a friend who has been so kind to him for the two and a half dreadful years that he was away.*
>
> *I do hope your father will allow you to travel to the*

depths of Wales to see us. We (my husband and I, Father and his second wife Lowri, and their child, Mari Elen, and particularly Miss Nano Rees, a woman in her late seventies who has been our greatest support for as many years as I can remember) do hope they will.

We look forward to meeting you. My husband could meet you at our local railway station, Llanfryn Carmarthenshire, at any time.

We look forward to hearing from you,

Yours faithfully,

Catrin Andrews.

'I'm Catrin Andrews,' she thought as she wrote her signature, 'how extraordinary. And my child will be either Thomas Joshua Andrews or Rachel Mary Andrews. I hope he or she decides to arrive soon. My body is so ungainly. I'm waddling like an old mother goose already. My thighs are huge and rub together whenever I move. Soon I shall be unable to walk at all.'

Miss May Malcolm spent no time in getting back in touch.

Thank you very much for your kind invitation. I'm delighted to hear that Tom is safe. I hadn't heard from him for several weeks and now, of course, I understand why. Please tell him that I look forward to seeing him and you all very soon. I would like to arrive on Friday evening on the seven fifty train. I trust that this will be convenient.

Tom became pale and agitated when Catrin read him the letter. 'What an ordeal for the poor girl,' he said. 'I wonder if she realises what a ruin of a man she's coming to meet.'

'Stop putting yourself down,' Catrin said. 'You're a handsome man in your prime and if she doesn't snap you up, there are plenty of young girls around here who will.'

'Certainly,' his father said. 'I'm sure a wounded soldier is high on the list of every young female of marriageable age. Our maids now, Lottie and Maudie, can't take their eyes off you and they're both handsome girls. You could do worse.'

'Well, Miss Rees,' Josi told Nano later that morning, 'May Malcolm is travelling all the way from London especially to see you on Friday evening. If you approve of her then I'm prepared to give her my blessing and Lowri's. Perhaps Hendre Ddu will have its first English mistress in its long history.'

'You won't hear me say a word against the English. There are plenty of Welshmen, and women too, who are far from perfect.'

'I agree with you there. I myself am one of them, but after a long period of remorse I am striving towards some form of inner peace.'

'You're a decent man, Mr Ifans, though I never thought you were good enough for my dearest Rachel.'

'I haven't slept a wink,' Tom confessed the next morning. 'I'm just not good enough for her. I'm sorry to be putting her through the ordeal of coming here and meeting us all.'

'What's wrong with us? We're a fairly civilised family and we have a lovely home. And I made it clear that you merely want to see her to resume your friendship. What sort of ordeal is that?'

'Oh, Catrin,' Lowri said, 'I think she's very brave to travel down here. I don't think I could do it even if I was in love with Mr Tom.' Lowri blushed as she realised what she'd said.

'I think you were a little in love with me once, Lowri,' Tom said, 'but then in my absence, my father stepped in and captured you for himself.'

On Friday morning, Graham Andrews joined them after his visit to Miss Rees. 'She's a different woman, this morning,' he said. 'She tells me that she means to get up in the afternoon to make some Welsh cakes and a few loaves of bara brith.'

'And will she?' Josi asked him.

'No,' he said, 'but it shows that she's rallying. She may last the summer yet. Of course you can depend on me to meet the seven-fifty train. Catrin, try not to over-do things today. With all the work I have in the hospital, I simply won't have time to deliver a baby this week. Take it easy, don't walk too far, don't eat too much and remember, nothing spiced.'

He kissed his wife and left them.

'I can handle the supper without any help from you,' Lowri said. 'We've got new potatoes and new beans and I'll start baking the ham – in brown sugar and honey – Nano's old recipe, later on this morning. Would you like to order a pudding, Tom? Maudie assures me she can manage the pudding.'

'Strawberry cheesecake and cream, I think,' Tom said after some serious deliberation.

Josi broke in. 'Tom, Graham's been having a word with me. He is adamant that the only way for you to stop having such dreadful nightmares is to share some of the horrors with us. I beg you to try, Tom. Not one of us is strong enough to put up with those terrible screams. It mustn't happen while May Malcolm is here. Why don't we go to sit in the orchard and you can try to talk things over with me. I'd like to help you, son, if I can.'

'Thank you, Father, but I think it's too soon,' Tom said. 'I'm going to try to fill my head with lovely country scenes today; the men haymaking, the women carrying out the tea trays and the larks singing. I don't believe in war today. When the bad times come again, as they will, I may well be glad to take up your offer.'

Mari Elen piped up. 'When you had that bad dream, Tom, I heard you and wet the bed. Father wasn't too pleased but Lowri said he was to go downstairs to fetch me a cup of milk and two biscuits. But he didn't bring the ones I like, the ones with pink icing on the top. It's not so good for me now that you are here and Miss Rees is ill.'

'Hadn't you better visit Miss Rees?' Lowri suggested, 'but remember you mustn't wake her if she's asleep.'

'I wonder if she would like some of those biscuits with pink icing on the top. Shall I look for some for her?'

'By all means,' Catrin said, 'Two for you and two for her, but no more.'

'Two is good but three is better,' Mari Elen said. 'All the same, two each. Thank you. And may I have some ginger beer from the pantry?'

Catrin sighed. 'I'll come with you to pour some. You've only just finished your breakfast Mari Elen. How can you be hungry again so soon?'

'I don't know.'

'Are you happy here?' Catrin asked her, 'or would you prefer to be home in Cefn Hebog?'

'I miss my pet duck and my dear little kitten. Dogs are all very well but they don't climb on your lap, do they, or sit on your head.'

'I'm sure we could fetch your kitten. I'll ask Graham to go up there tomorrow morning.'

Poor Graham had a hard time as he drove May from the station that evening; she seemed too shy to speak a word. Was she apprehensive or merely exhausted after the journey? He felt the ordeal of meeting the family would really finish her off. How had Tom managed to elicit the promise of writing from such a very shy girl? His admiration for his brother-in-law increased. He was determined that he and Catrin would return to their home that evening after supper, so that there should only be Josi, Lowri and Tom himself left there. He hoped Mari Elen would already have been put to bed, but knew that there was little chance of that; not one of them would have managed to send her upstairs. He was fond enough of Mari Elen but he seemed to be the only one – with the possible exception of Miss Rees – who was aware of how strong minded and spoilt she was. He hoped Catrin would not be as indulgent towards their own child. He had been brought up in a very strict Scottish manse where children were never asked what they wanted to do, but very firmly told what was expected of them.

He pulled up in front of the house so that May could appreciate what a beautiful place it was. She looked up at the old bricks, a rosy pink in the sun-drenched evening and gasped. 'I never expected this,' she said. 'From his letters, I thought Tom lived in quite a modest farmhouse. This is really beautiful.'

He took her in by the front door and into the parlwr. There was no sign of anyone. He pushed open the door into the dining room, the table was not even laid.

At that moment Lowri flew downstairs. She greeted May with great warmth as though they were already firm friends. 'Catrin is having her baby,' she told them. 'Yes, it's all started and we're all so excited. Tom has been sitting with her while Josi was out finishing the milking but now that you're back, Tom can come down. I'll fetch him,' she told May. 'Can I take your coat? I'm so sorry I don't seem to have anything done so far. We've all been up with Catrin. She's in one of her funny moods. She's not really so far on in labour as she thinks, apparently it's only just beginning. But at the moment she wants all of us with her, she says. Mrs Ifans, Mrs Evans I mean, her mother, used to say she was as highly strung as a prize-winning filly. Whenever she was going out to a party or a ball I was sent to sit with her all the afternoon and we used to have a lovely time dressing up and trying out different hairstyles. Oh, I'm talking too much, I'm excited as well. I'll send Tom now. He can't manage the stairs very well,' she told May, 'but you'll understand that, I know. Shall I take you to the bathroom? Or to your bedroom?'

'No, I'll wait here for Tom,' she said. 'And please give Catrin my best wishes.'

Before Tom had got down, Josi arrived from the kitchen and introduced himself. 'Would you like to come up to see Catrin?' he asked her. 'I know she's longing to see you. And don't worry, I don't think the baby will be born today or even tomorrow morning. Catrin is just enjoying all the attention. I don't think she's had one proper pain yet, but I don't like to tell her that.'

Tom arrived downstairs and Lowri and Josi excused themselves and returned to Catrin. 'What a lovely girl,' Lowri said. 'What are we going to give her for supper? I think it will have to be ham sandwiches and I haven't had time to bake any bread today so it'll have to be ham sandwiches with yesterday's bread. But she'll understand won't she? She seems like family already.'

'She looks so like Rachel when I first met her. Tom is marrying his mother, I'm afraid. He always doted on her.'

'No, he told me that you were the one who meant most to him but that Catrin was always your favourite.'

'Nonsense, nonsense,' Josi said, 'I was nothing to him. He was a Morgan, through and through. Catrin, I really think you ought to get up. Lying in bed will only slow down your delivery. I know about these things. Take cows now, they're always better off if they stand up and try to munch a little hay.'

'I'm not a cow,' Catrin wailed.

'No, but we're not so far from the animal world as some people like to think. Elephants, for instance, now they have all the aunties crowding round during a birth. Listen, I know what I'm talking about. And when the matriarch of the herd dies, they have a real family funeral with ham sandwiches and stewed black tea. Mari Elen was given a book about elephants and I know all about them.'

'I don't know as much as you do about animals,' Graham said. 'But I've been saying much the same thing to her, and I can't get her to move. She wants us all to have supper up here but I'm begging her to think of May Malcolm who's so shy and will cope better with a formal meal.'

'There won't be much of a formal meal though, I'm afraid,' Lowri said. 'I've been trying to get away to get the vegetables cooked, but Catrin keeps on begging me to stay here to dab cologne on her forehead.'

'Mari Elen, go down to say hello to your new auntie and then please go to bed. It's very late for you to be up.'

Mari Elen looked at Graham in some alarm. 'I'm much too useful here,' she said. 'Catrin wouldn't hear of my leaving her when she may be dying. Mrs Prosser's sister died in childbirth, you know,' she told him crossly, 'I heard her telling Miss Rees about it. I'm staying here even if no one brings me any supper like a ham sandwich with some pickle and some of Miss Rees' ginger beer. I've also promised Miss Rees to let her know exactly what is going on. I'm being kept very busy you know.'

'You're only three years old and it's now time for your

bed. Say goodnight to Catrin and ask Lowri to get you a bite of supper in the kitchen.'

Mari Elen, looking martyred, was so surprised by Graham that she went off without further word. Josi, looking admiringly at his son-in-law, followed her. 'We have to do exactly what the doctor orders today,' he explained to Mari Elen. 'May, this is my daughter who wants to say goodnight to you before she goes to the kitchen to have her supper.'

'Hello May,' Mari Elen said. 'I hear that you are Tom's young lady. I hope you like it here.'

'I really do. And I shall look forward to seeing you again tomorrow. Goodnight, little girl.'

'Nos da,' Mari Elen said. 'And cysgwch yn dawel. That means good night and sleep well.'

'Thank you. I hope you teach me a few words of Welsh before I leave here. "Nos da," that's my first bit. Goodnight.'

'I'll take you upstairs to see Miss Rees now,' Josi said, 'and you can say that to her.'

'Well, Tom,' Lowri said, 'we all like your Miss Malcolm. Are you happy?'

'Yes,' Tom said, 'Oh yes, I really am. But I wish she wouldn't go on talking about my being a hero. It's deeply embarrassing. I can't tell you how nervous and frightened I really was. Whenever I had to sleep in the trench, my greatcoat on a layer of wet mud and knowing I had to be responsible for a company of men in a few hours, do you know, the only way I could get to sleep was to pretend that I was camping in the orchard as I used to when I was a boy. That's pathetic isn't it? In a grown man.'

'Not at all, it's very sensible if you ask me, letting the mind help the body in those terrible circumstances. Very sensible.'

They all, including Catrin, gathered in the dining room to have supper. Lowri seemed to have found a great array of salad and pickles to accompany the baked ham and everyone ate heartily except for Catrin who wouldn't have anything except bread and honey.

'I feel as though I've entered into the set of a theatre play,' May said, 'in this beautiful dining room with all your worthy ancestors looking down at us so seriously. One person home from war, one person about to give birth, the family servant trying to decide whether to get up tomorrow or carry on with dying since everyone is expecting it, and a hint of thunder in the air. It's very exciting… I honestly don't usually talk as much as this on first getting to know people, but you see I feel I know all of you already from Tom's letters: Catrin so beautiful, Lowri so lovely and so calm and kind, who's been apologising to me about one of the nicest suppers I've ever eaten, his handsome father whom he idolised as a child and Miss Rees who I hope will decide to live so that I can get to know her. Oh, please, you must all forgive me if I seem over-familiar.'

'You're not at all over-familiar, you're just being friendly. And we all hope to have another cause for celebration very soon. I mean as well as the new baby,' Josi said.

After that, no one said anything for a long time.

Chapter four

It was almost five the next morning. 'It's a girl,' Mari Elen pronounced, waking Lowri by pulling hard at her eyelashes. 'It's a girl. Catrin's new baby, it's a girl. I was the first to see her because I went along to Catrin's bedroom as soon as I woke up and the little baby was only half an hour old. She's not very beautiful but Graham says she'll improve in a day or two, and Lowri, Catrin is dying for a really thick ham sandwich with some jelly in it and a whole egg custard and two pints of water. That's what she's asked for. But first of all she wants you to go along to see the new baby. Even though you may be disappointed: she's not very beautiful at the moment, a little curled-up face with wet hair, and she doesn't stop mewing like a very tiny kitten.'

Lowri jumped out of bed pulling on her clothes without bothering to wash or comb her hair. 'Oh, Catrin, she's so beautiful. She looks just like you. Can I hold her? Oh, Catrin you must be so happy.'

'I am so happy, Lowri, though I kept dreaming of Edward during the time I was half asleep and half awake last night. I hope Graham didn't hear me calling for him, though I think he realises how I still feel. Please Lowri ask him to come back to see me before he goes out to work. He has to make a very early start today because of people he failed to see last night. He's gone to the small spare room at the moment, trying to get some sleep for a couple of hours. I think May's lovely don't you Lowri? What did my father say about her?'

'He thinks she looks like Rachel when he first met her so I suppose he must think her very special. I'm going to tell Miss Rees about the new arrival and then I'll bring you a very large breakfast. Shall I leave Mari Elen here with you? Then you can send her to fetch whoever you want to see. Who would you like to see?'

'Oh, everyone. I want everyone here to see my gorgeous baby as soon as possible. Is Tom awake yet? Is May?'

'I'll send them up as soon as they appear for breakfast. But cariad, it's not half past five yet.'

'Oh, Lowri I'm so happy.'

Catrin was happy and so was the entire family, hers was the first baby of the younger generation.

'You said you intended to call the baby Rachel Mary,' Tom said, when he visited her after breakfast. 'Is there any special reason for the Mary? Obviously Rachel is for Mother and it's a lovely name as well. But Mary?'

'No special reason but both Graham and I thought it sounded good with Rachel.'

'So it does, but so does May. Would Rachel May be at all feasible as an alternative?'

'Rachel May. Yes that sounds lovely. Though of course it's mid June now. But all the same it's a lovely name.'

'You see, May has promised to marry me and it would be such a happy way to remember our happiness and our engagement. And it would ensure that the baby has a very special place in her rich uncle's affections.'

'You intend to be a rich uncle, then? I'm very glad to hear it.'

'Yes, I'm anxious to study farming properly and to find better ways of cultivating the land and raising stock. Graham was giving me some interesting points on the way Scottish farmers have developed and diversified mixed farming. We mustn't go on and on in the old style without any experimentation. I hope to interest Father in some of my new ideas.'

'He may well be anxious to get back to Cefn Hebog, though, Tom. He loves Cefn Hebog and, as you know, regards it as his rightful inheritance.'

'He must stay here with me for the time being. He can get a manager to look after Cefn Hebog. It feels so right that we are all here together. After all, there's plenty of room here.'

It wasn't to be. Over lunch Graham said that he would be taking Catrin and the baby home with him as soon as it was feasible. 'I've arranged for the district nurse to call in every morning,' he told Tom, 'and of course I'll see you every evening when I call in to see Miss Rees. Lowri has too much work already without our adding to her burdens. I have a capable housekeeper and a little nursemaid, Molly Price, the youngest daughter of Ted and Alice Price, Gors Las, to care for Catrin and our daughter.'

'Our daughter,' said Catrin. 'Doesn't that sound delightful? I agree that Lowri already has too much to do, looking after the family and Miss Rees. And the nurse. I wish I could help you cariad, but Graham says I mustn't do too much or I shall lose my milk. I know Graham will be happy to bring us over every Sunday to lunch. By the way, Graham, I haven't given you today's good news. Tom has asked May to marry him and she's agreed to it. They are now officially engaged and we can expect an invitation to the wedding very soon.'

'I'm delighted with your news,' Graham said to Tom. 'I half expected it because I could sense how happy you were to find each other again.'

'Mari Elen has been told the news already,' Josi said. 'She's extremely interested in holy matrimony and is already wondering who there is for her. Mrs Prosser has only two girls which is very disappointing.'

'Don't be silly, Dada, I'm going to marry the Prince of Wales.'

'Have you heard that our little daughter is to be called Rachel May?' Graham asked May.

'Oh, how wonderful,' she said, blushing prettily. 'I shall do my best to deserve the honour.'

'And Miss Rees says the baby looks the image of Mother,' Catrin said. 'That is the greatest compliment she can bestow. She looked after Mother for fifty years, May, and in all that time she never did anything to offend her except marrying Father who was not nearly good enough for her. However, he was forgiven as soon as Tom was born, because of course Tom was the handsomest baby ever born, nine and a half pounds in weight and with an expression wise as a preacher.'

'Catrin you're getting over-excited,' Graham said. 'Tomorrow I'll take you home, put you straight to bed and send Molly up to look after you.'

Catrin stood up meekly and went back to bed as though she realised that she was over-tiring herself.

'You will come over to see us?' she asked May and Tom.

'Of course. We'll hire a car and come over before the end of the week. We must take care of our little niece.'

'She was getting over-excited,' Lowri said. 'Her cheeks were flushed and her eyes were too bright. I always recognise the signs. She'll have one of her headaches before evening. Excuse me now, I must see if Miss Rees has managed to eat anything. By the way, she's decided to stay with us at least until Michaelmas when it will be easier for us to hire another housekeeper. We have to go to her for our instructions every morning and she vows that she'll be up by the end of the week. Though Dr Andrews, Graham I mean, doesn't think she'll ever leave her bed.'

'Oh, that's too cruel,' Tom said. 'I can't imagine this place without Miss Rees at the helm. How will we manage without her? Have you any idea, Lowri?'

'She'll be hard to replace. Perhaps I ought to ask Mrs Prosser whether she knows of any hard-working widow who might like the job along with a good home. I can't think of anyone except possibly…'

'Except possibly who?'

'Well,' Lowri hesitated, glancing over at Josi for support, 'an aunt of mine has recently been widowed and she's very restless and nervous on her own. I think she'd jump at the chance to come here, at least for a trial period. Of course we'd have to tell Miss Rees that it was a temporary appointment.'

'Oh, do ask her Lowri. Anyone in your family would be dependable, we know that,' Catrin said.

'And hard-working,' Josi added. 'And I think she's probably my second cousin as well, and when did anyone from my family let us down?'

'We certainly can't manage on our own,' said Catrin. 'I feel awful that we have to depend on Lowri to do everything.'

'There isn't too much to do, honestly. I don't like being idle. I was never one to sit with my hands in my lap all afternoon. I wasn't brought up to be a grand lady. You see, I've come up in the world,' she told May. 'I'll tell you all about it one day.'

Chapter five

The next day brought very sad news. Old Sarah Morris, once a maid at Hendre Ddu, had heard that her second son, Dewi, had been killed in action. She'd already lost her eldest son, Gethyn Wyn. Josi and Tom decided to go to visit Sarah, taking her some money for the funeral tea.

They found the house empty with no one there to open the door or ask them in. At last the woman next door saw them there and came to speak to them. 'Ever since she heard the news, Sarah spends all her time in the woods,' she said. 'She seems to gain some strength by being on her own. She might come home to have a bite of dinner with me, but she eats less than a child. What is to become of her? She lived for those two sons. She'll never be able to manage the smallholding on her own.'

'We'll wait here until she comes home,' Josi said. 'Though I don't know how anyone can comfort her.'

They were soon joined by Mr Isaacs, the minister, who'd only that morning heard of the tragedy. 'Poor soul, what will she do?' he asked them. 'She's not at all strong and won't be able to manage this little place on her own. She's almost sixty – she was late having her children – and her only daughter died of TB before the war started. She was a dear sweet creature, Myfanwy, pretty as a flower, but she passed away at eighteen and now here's a further tragedy. War is particularly hard on poor people who can't afford hired help. I'm glad you're here. Having visitors is bound to keep her busy making tea for a short time at least. And because you are here, I think I'll decide to leave and come back this evening. You can tell her that I'll be along as soon as I've had my supper at half past six. My wife will send her some supper too, I daresay.'

After Mr Isaacs had left, the next-door neighbour came out again. 'My big worry is that she'll do away with herself,' she told them. 'I've heard her say that she'll never be able to manage on her own. D'you know she left the house at eight this morning, what can she be doing? It's almost midday now. I wonder if we ought to go out to search for her?'

'I think we should,' Josi said. 'It's a gorgeous morning, I can't bear to think of her thinking of suicide, though one couldn't blame her. The last of her three fine children gone. It seems too hard.'

They entered the thick woods which were a dark emerald green that morning, the sun only fitfully able to penetrate the foliage. They listened as they walked, hoping to hear the sounds of someone crying, someone lamenting, but there was no sound. They came to the river. 'Gwynfor's boy is a fine swimmer,' Josi said. 'Perhaps I'll go to Fron Isa to see if I can bring him back with me. He'd enjoy a dip on a morning like this. I've never been a swimmer and I'd drown if I were to try to swim in that current.'

Josi went off and Tom was left alone on the bank, feeling sure that the tragedy of war was going to claim another victim. How could poor Sarah go on? She was a widow, very frail she looked, her only relations living in North Wales. What had she been doing since eight o'clock that morning?

There were no birds singing, no noise of any sort to be heard. Tom wished he had brought some paper and a pencil. As a boy he had loved drawing woods and the river and his mother had thought that he and Catrin had real talent. She herself had drawn and painted as a young girl and had always supplied them with expensive drawing paper and paint. For a moment he forgot the tragedy around him and wondered if he could make a livelihood as an artist as he was obviously unable to be a working farmer. He remembered drawing and painting with Edward when he was at university. They had joined a sketching club and had both enjoyed drawing the beautiful buildings and bridges of Oxford. As always there was a hard pain in his chest as he thought of Edward, who had been killed on the first day of the Ypres Offensive, the worst day of the war according to some.

Josi returned with young Gwyn. 'I've told him what he's to look for, but he's a brave lad and he's ready for it. The lad's got relations at New Quay and they all swim like seals there, he'll be fine. Just look at the banks as you swim along, lad, the places where a body might be held up by branches or weeds. If she's in the river, she won't have gone far.' Josi's eyes misted over, remembering Miriam's suicide and the end of his happiness. He had pictured her a hundred times thrown onto some outcrop and half-covered over with seaweed. He was convinced that Gwyn would find Sarah in very much the same position. Tom put his arm on his shoulder. 'Black days,' he said, his voice full of sympathy. 'I've had some, too, Tada.'

After about ten minutes of anxious waiting, Gwyn returned with grim news. He had found Sarah Morris' body and she was dead. 'She was quite dead, Mr Ifans, but she looked very peaceful; at first I thought she was smiling at me.' The boy came out of the water and burst into tears.

'Good boy,' Josi said, 'good brave boy. When you're dressed I've got half a crown here for you to slip into your pocket. You've done well.'

'She was very kind to me, Mr Ifans,' Gwyn said. 'She let me borrow Dewi's bicycle more than once. This war is a bloody old thing isn't it?'

'You're right,' Tom said. 'That's what it is, a bloody old thing. And here's half a crown from me as well.'

They walked down to where the lad had found the body and then waited for Davy Prosser and Ifan Walter to help them carry it back to the cottage. They were all quiet, even instructions were whispered. The woman next door came out to give them cups of tea and to say she would lay out the body. Tom wished he was young enough to burst into tears and howl with grief as Gwyn had done. The war is a bloody old thing isn't it, he thought.

The funeral was well attended, everyone from the three parishes seemed to have turned up to show their sympathy with the poor widow who had found life too much for her. Mr Isaacs made no reference to the fact that suicide was a considered a sin against God. On the contrary, he seemed full of sympathy and pity for the poor woman.

He prayed for her and for her young soldier son whose life had ended almost before it began. He was only nineteen and a popular, lusty, curly haired boy, always ready for any mischief or prank.

Mr Isaacs reported that Dewi was the seventh young soldier to be killed from their small parish. 'It's the fourth year of the war. They've taken our horses and they've taken our young men. How long, oh Lord, how long.' By the last hymn, many people were in tears.

A young relation from North Wales, a Miss Tudor, came down to take over Sarah's cottage. Fair play to her, she found the money to pay for the shroud and the coffin and for the funeral tea. On the next Sunday, Mr Isaacs introduced her to the congregation as Sarah's niece and it was learnt later that she was a dressmaker and that she would be living in the cottage and was hoping that people would be pleased with her fine workmanship and fair prices.

Catrin was one of her first customers. She had bought a length of crimson slub silk in Carmarthen and wanted it made into a dress. Miss Tudor seemed to have no patterns but she knew exactly what Cartrin wanted, took measurements and would like a fitting in a week's time when it would be cut out and tacked. The cost was not mentioned.

'What is she like, this Miss Tudor?' Lowri asked.

'She's small as a child and she has brown hair pulled severely away from her face. She looks like an industrious little mouse. I hope she's a good dressmaker. I paid a lot for that silk.'

By the following week she had found out that Miss Tudor was not a good dressmaker. She was in tears when Catrin turned up to fit the new dress and confessed that she had never before worked as a dressmaker, but had thought it would be much easier than it was. 'I've always been good at making clothes for my dolls,' she said, sniffing into a minute lace handkerchief. 'My stitching is very fine, but I didn't realise how difficult it would be to cut out shapes for grown-ups. Please don't be cross with me.'

The beautiful silk was spoilt. Luckily Catrin found her story so amusing that she wasn't as indignant as she might have been.

'Could you let me have just a little money?' Miss Tudor asked. 'I did try my best. I was up until three o'clock this morning altering and trying different things. If I had some money I'd go back home and try to learn dressmaking as my mother wanted me to.'

'I couldn't refuse to pay her,' Catrin told Lowri later that day. 'She doesn't seem to have any money. I've asked Graham to call there to take her to the station next week. I won't tell him that she's ruined my lovely material.'

'I think you have enough left to make a skirt,' Lowri

said. 'It's only the bodice she's ruined. Shall I try to make you a nice full skirt? You could wear it with that cream Chantilly lace blouse you have. And I won't charge you anything.'

'Thank you, love,' Catrin said. 'I can't help thinking about little Miss Tudor. I promised to go back there if she comes back when she's done her apprenticeship.'

She never came back and the small cottage stood empty for years.

Chapter six

When Graham next came over to the farm, he sat alone with Josi for a long time

Josi told them all later that Catrin had fallen into a serious depression after her excitement over her brother's return from France and the baby's birth. Apparently the medical profession had recently been made aware of a phenomenon described as post-natal depression which was a serious illness and could well last for some months, even years, and in the worse cases for a whole lifetime.

After taking advice from doctors who had experienced such a phenomenon, he had decided that the best course of action was to bring Catrin and the baby back to Hendre Ddu where she had her family to turn to, rather than to leave her alone all day while he was out seeing his patients. 'She can bring Molly, the little nanny, with her to attend to the baby and to take over some of the night nursing, while I keep the housekeeper to look after me.'

Josi, of course, said that they would all be very pleased to help in any way they could and would be delighted to welcome Catrin and the baby whenever it was convenient.

'Now,' he said seriously to Mari Elen, 'do you think you can be a really good girl while Catrin is with us. She's not well and needs rest with no shouting or bad behaviour.'

'I'll try to be very good,' she promised. 'But if people are unreasonable towards me and treat me as a child, then, of course, it's very difficult for me. It's hardly my fault if Miss Rees thinks I'm too young to hear anything she has to say and sends me downstairs to fetch her a glass of water when she already has a full jug of fresh water on her side table. I promise to be good if people are good to me.'

'But cariad, you are a child and people don't want to burden you with grown-up troubles you can't understand. But come and tell me or Lowri if you think people are being unreasonable to you, instead of screaming and kicking. Do you promise? Catrin is quite seriously ill and we must all be very careful of her. May is returning to London very soon, but she's going to make arrangements for the wedding and after that she will be returning here to be mistress of Hendre Ddu. I heard a whisper last night that she may be asking you to be her bridesmaid, which will mean a lovely new dress and a crown of flowers. I shouldn't really have told you that, but you see I want you to be happy.'

'I hope pink rosebuds, then, for the headdress. And I think I'd better choose the dress I want so that Auntie May won't choose anything babyish.'

'Heaven forbid,' Josi muttered. He often felt too old to be a father of someone so very young and new as Mari

Elen. He also felt that he would far better understand a little lad. Women were a mystery. Catrin had been so excited and happy to be a new mother and now she was 'seriously depressed'. Perhaps she needed a glimpse of the real world where women had babies without the means to care for them. He had seen cases of frightful poverty, but not, thank God, amongst the workers at Hendre Ddu.

Lowri was clearly the best companion for Catrin. The two were almost the same age and had always been firm friends. 'You must now forget all the work that you normally do and concentrate on being with Catrin,' Josi told her. 'You can leave everything else, particularly caring for Miss Rees, to the new nurse. She seems so capable. Well, of course she is. Dr Andrews would have made sure of that.'

Tom and May seemed to drift about the farm in a daze of happiness. Tom was learning to walk with a walking stick instead of a crutch and never mentioned his misfortune in losing his leg. 'On the contrary I regard it as the greatest good luck. I got out of that hell hole before being thrown out for attempting a mutiny. I wish someone would.'

'What would your father, the colonel, think of my son's cheerful insubordination?'

'I think he has some ideas of what a fearful carnage the war is turning into. All the same, I shall certainly advise Tom to keep his thoughts to himself when he comes home to ask for my hand.'

That evening Lowri was unable to join the company for supper. Catrin was strruggling to feed the baby and Lowri was up with her, trying to get the tiny girl to take a few drops of nourishment from a spoon, all of them weeping.

'I'm not having a baby when I grow up. They're too much trouble and they cry too much. I think the one we've got is rather bad tempered and spoilt,' Mari Elen said.

'Has Lowri always been Catrin's best friend?' May cut in tactfully.

'Yes. Lowri is a relative of mine, a second cousin I believe, and when she came here as a servant we impressed on both Catrin and Tom that they were to think of her as a cousin and not merely as a maid.'

'We've always had that easy relationship with all the servants here,' Tom added. 'In Wales most of us like to think that we're all more or less one class. When a lad is hired at Michaelmas to be the junior in a farm – "gwas bach" we call him, "the little lad" – it's very rare for him to leave the family afterwards, he shares their poverty in the hard times, and shares their meals in the kitchen until he's too old to work and then retires to one of the cottages. It's almost unheard of for him to try to better himself by moving to another farm and it's a disgrace to the family if that happens. It means he was treated badly. But most often the sons of the house and the 'gwas' are firm friends. The very word "gwas" can't be translated as "servant" but as "lad".

'I have to admit that it's very different in England,' May replied. 'I've been to stay in one or two very grand houses with some of the friends I went to school with, and there the servants are trained to turn round to face the wall if they come across any of the family in any of the passages. I always found it very embarrassing.'

Josi and Tom looked at each other in amazement. 'It's no wonder that the Russians are planning a revolution,' Tom said. 'If I were a serf and treated like that I'd certainly be one of the revolutionaries and prepared to give my life for the cause.'

'And I wouldn't blame you, son.'

'But there's unrest in the army too, so many of the rank and file are suspicious and antagonistic towards their officers. Believe me there'll be a great upheaval when the war is finally over. During my time in France, well over two and a half years, I came across dozens, perhaps hundreds of South Wales miners or sons of mining families. Oh, they swear and spit and speak a comedy type of bastardised English, all "butty" and "duw-duw"and "mynufferni", but they're all intelligent and very politically aware. Their leaders are sent to Ruskin College by the Working Men's Union and they come back Marxists to a man and they all seem to be waiting for a class war. Of course they regarded me as bit of a joke, but at least I managed to convince them that I was no spy and eventually they recognised that I was passionately interested in what they had to say.'

'I can understand what you're saying, Tom. But I do hope there'll be no revolution in England. Think of all the bloodshed and mindless killing in France in the eighteenth century.'

'Yes. But there was never quite as much inequality afterwards. It prevented the rich becoming ever richer and the poor being left to starve. The conditions in France before the revolution were indescribably vile. Anyway, all

I'm ever likely to do is talk. I'm very unlikely to take part in any earth-shattering events. I've had enough of action for the remainder of my life. I couldn't ever be a Marxist anyway; it's too extreme and too idealistic. I mean, take the best of our chapel people, those who really believe in the Sermon on the Mount, are there any that really give all their money to the poor? Or even share it with the poor? As Christians, we know what to do but haven't the will to do it and I think Marxism would be exactly the same. I think the most resonant verse in the Bible is when God, having sent the great flood to punish the sinners in Noah's time, sets the rainbow in the sky as a solemn promise that it would never happen again, having realised that "man is evil in his heart". That's a hard truth, but it needs to be accepted so that we don't become too idealistic. All the same, there certainly needs to be something in between man's highest ideals and the greed of our present institutions.'

'We never know what we might be called upon to do. Some form of socialism certainly attracts me,' Josi said. 'But I don't think we ought to carry on like this or May may well regret her decision to become engaged to you.'

'No I won't,' May said. 'I have great interest and absolute trust in your opinions, both of you.'

Josi was pleased to notice that May's friendship with Lowri did not alter in any way after being informed of her humble origins.

Lowri's aunt was soon running the house efficiently and smoothly.

Miss Rees was unable to be very civil to her despite being told that she was there in a temporary capacity. 'No,' she said sadly, 'she's my replacement. My days of running Hendre Ddu are over and though I may get a little better, I shall never again be as I was. I've known too many people with strokes, it's a very popular illness in this part of Wales. Yes, they may get better, but they never get well. Never mind, I've lived long enough to meet the new mistress of Hendre Ddu and if I'm very lucky I may live long enough to see the new heir.'

She wasn't to have her wish. The very next morning when Lowri took her an early cup of tea, she found the old woman dead. It was possible that she had died in her sleep. But Lowri felt it was much more likely that she had been fully conscious, waiting for death to overtake her but choosing not to trouble anyone. The bell left with her was safely at her side, but she had obviously scorned to call for help. For a time, Catrin sat at her side, crying. She was sure Tom would be equally affected. Nano was such an important part of their lives, had been with them from the beginning.

Even though Dr Andrews had warned them of the possibility, they were all stunned by the news. Breakfast that morning was a very difficult meal, the time-honoured clichés were trotted out, even Josi being too upset to eat his usual three courses.

During the next few days though, everyone was busy preparing for the funeral which had to be magnificent to reflect the position Miss Rees had held in the family. Lowri's aunt, Mrs Hopkins, seemed the most ardent that everything should be seen at its best and as she'd been hired to take over Miss Rees' position, it pleased her vanity to make sure that everyone should see what an honour it was. Maud and Lottie were kept busy from morning to night polishing the oak staircase, the floor of the hall and dining room as well as the tables and sideboards, while she and Lowri took over the vast amount of cooking she thought necessary. 'My little niece, Sali, is free at the moment,' she told Tom. 'May I give her a job for the duration of the funeral?'

'By all means,' Tom said. 'I liked little Sali. She was such a frightened child when I left here after my mother's funeral. Why did she leave?'

Mrs Hopkins had no idea, but Lowri and Catrin knew that she had offended Miss Rees in some way, though they hadn't been given any details. Lowri, in particular, was uneasy that she was being brought back; she tried to love her young sister as she loved her older siblings, but knew her to be flighty and rather sly. She hadn't managed to keep a place long after Miss Rees had dismissed her because other housekeepers knew that it wasn't something Miss Rees did without good and sufficient reason.

May got up on the morning of the funeral and marvelled at Hendre Ddu's beauty. The sun was shining in through huge elm trees around, leaving dappled shadows on the highly polished furniture, and fusing with the old Persian rugs. Looking out of the window, she thought the garden seemed newly polished too, each flower, each blade of grass bright with dew and sunshine.

'You've made the place look really splendid Mrs Hopkins,' she told the new housekeeper when she passed her after breakfast. 'May I pick some of the cream roses to put in the hall and the dining room?'

'Thank you, Miss Malcolm, I was hoping that someone would offer their services. I'm too impatient to be a good flower arranger.'

'And I'm sure you have far too much to do this morning. I'll just have time before we leave for chapel.'

Miss Rees' death had added to Catrin's sadness. 'What's the matter with me, Lowri?' Catrin asked her friend. 'I have everything to make me happy: my darling little longed-for baby and a good caring husband, and yet I feel as though my whole world is crumbling apart. Am I going mad, Lowri?'

'No, cariad. If anything it's because you married too soon after your terrible loss and sadness about Edward. I shall always remember how you loved him. I shall always remember the look you gave him on the day he left here, I recognised it as the sort of love that only the few know. Maybe if you confessed your feeling to Graham – he's an understanding man I think – he would be very sympathetic; and if you talked openly about it you'd feel much better very soon.'

'But could I expect his sympathy? Won't he think that I had no right to marry him when my heart was so bruised?'

'I don't think so. Be honest with him. He wanted you, had to have you, bruised or not. I'm sure that telling him how you feel is the best thing you can do. Come along now, cariad, we have to go.'

Graham was taking Tom, May, Catrin and Lowri in his motor car while Josi, Mari Elen and most of the farm servants had already started on their walk. Lowri wished that she and Catrin had time to walk to chapel, feeling that the arches of wild roses and honeysuckle in the hedges would weave their way into Catrin's sore heart.

'I wish you'd carry on with your painting, Catrin,' she told her in the car.

'You – and Tom – had such talent. I think I'll get your paints out tomorrow and lock you into the office until you've painted me a picture. I'd love a painting of wild roses for my sitting room in Cefn Hebog. I'd like to show you Cefn Hebog, May. It's been in Josi's family since the seventeenth century. It's not a bit grand like Hendre Ddu, well, the exact opposite perhaps, but I think you'd like it.'

'I'm sure I would. When will you take me? I'd love a good long walk one afternoon.'

'And it's the best time of the year, isn't it? May and June and early July?'

The little chapel was completely full by the time they arrived, so that many of the congregation had to remain outside. Still, the weather was perfect, neither too hot nor too cold. The minister told the congregation after the last hymn had been sung that everyone was welcome at Hendre Ddu following the service.

It was the singing that had impressed May. She knew that Welsh people were noted for their love of singing, but was still surprised that an ordinary, though very large, chapel congregation could, without rehearsal, sound so like a great, well-trained choir. Such grand laments, she wished she could understand the words but could only remember two or three words of the last haunting hymn, 'Mor dawel yw'; she'd ask Tom to translate them for her as soon as they were alone. The whole hour and a half service was almost unbearably moving with Mari Elen's occasional loud sobbing only adding to the emotion of the occasion.

Back at Hendre Ddu, the sadness seemed to have evaporated and everyone spoke of and joked about 'the dear departed' as though she was still with them. Rachel had had Miss Rees' portrait painted on her fiftieth birthday and people raised their glasses to her likeness and spoke of her loyalty, her generosity and her abrupt dealings with anyone she thought had proved less than loyal to the family.

The food shortages of the third year of war were hardly felt in the bigger farms of West Wales and were certainly not allowed to impinge on the important occasions. The great joints of ham and beef, the pickles, the cold new potatoes and momentous fresh salads soon disappeared, along with the huge flagons of home-made cider and ginger beer.

The minister spoke: 'In chapel I respectfully spoke of Miss Hannah Rees. But I wonder how many of you thought of her as Miss Hannah Rees? No, she was Nano, Hendre Ddu to everyone in the three parishes. She lost her name in the service of this family whom she loved and served so well. And in fact I don't think she ever thought of herself as a servant but almost as the spirit of the house. She knew its history back to the seventeenth century and if you weren't very, very careful she'd have taken you back four generations while she was making you a cup of tea. The Thomas Morgan who had carried out the restoration of the old farm house, the Walter Morgan who had planted the trees in Pen Gwaelod, the Griffydd Morgan who had drained Hendre Isa, the Thomas Morgan who had built the chapel at Garmon. Let us celebrate her love and service, her great heart.'

'Thank you, Mrs Hopkins,' Tom said after all the guests had finally departed. 'Miss Rees would have been proud of the effort you've made.'

'No she wouldn't,' Mrs Hopkins said. 'She'd have been furious with me for trying to match her hospitality. I can just hear her now, "And who does she think she is? That no-good upstart thinking she can take my place, fill my shoes?" To tell you the truth I've been feeling very uncomfortable all day.'

Tom smiled but didn't argue with her. He realised that the new housekeeper knew Miss Rees almost as well as he did. 'We must clear out her room very soon so that you can have it. I think she told Catrin who in the family was to have her particular treasures and she mentioned a first cousin in Tregaron too, I believe. Lowri, do you remember her instructions? I don't think we can bother Catrin at the moment.'

'No. But I can help auntie see to it after we've got everything straight in the dining room and the parlwr.'

'Dear Lowri, what would we do without you? All the same, I'm sure you're longing to get back to the peace of Cefn Hebog.'

'No, no, this is my place at the moment, I know that.'

It was the evening after the funeral and Graham had found time to visit his wife and baby. 'I think Catrin's a little better than she was,' he told Tom. 'She's managing to feed the baby quite well now. She doesn't say much but at least she doesn't seem as restless and hopeless as she was. The mind is completely inexplicable, apparently, even to those who've spent a lifetime studying it. I've been reading articles about the treatment they're now giving soldiers whose nerves have failed them.'

'Is that so? From what I understood they were simply shot as deserters.'

'Oh, come now, I suppose some escaped that fate. Perhaps they were wounded in action before their nervous attacks.'

'Yes. Well, that's what happened to me, I suppose. Believe me, no one will get out of those trenches in one piece. I lost a leg, but I don't suppose I'll ever be free of my memories. I don't suppose any of us will.'

'But isn't there anyone you can talk to? I'm ready to listen, so is your father, I know.'

'One day, it may be easier. At the moment, to talk is to re-live and I'm not ready for that.'

Neither of them had noticed that Lowri was back in the room. Worry about Catrin had made her bold. 'You need to talk, too,' she told Graham. 'I think Catrin would be easier in her mind if you made her talk to you. And the only way she will is if you broached the subject and encouraged her.'

Both men looked at her with grave attention.

'I find it very difficult to talk about feelings,' Graham confessed. 'All the same, I think perhaps you're right, Lowri. Well, I'm sure of it. Of course Catrin realises that I know about her love for Edward, how could I help it when I saw how she suffered when she got the news of his death? All the same, I will make an effort to bring up the subject again, I really will. I'm determined to do everything I can to help her.'

The three of them sat without the energy to talk further. 'We seem to have had so much happening to us in such a short space of time,' Lowri said at last. 'I'd like a few quiet weeks now, with nothing to disturb us but the gradual unfolding of the seasons.'

Josi came in from the milking seeming as tired as the others. 'Well,' he said, 'Prosser asked me to tell you all that everyone he spoke to had appreciated the funeral dinner yesterday. But he wanted to remind me, very respectfully, that one thing had been overlooked. The young master's mother – it took me a few moments to work out he meant Rachel – would have been distributing whatever change, the copper and the small silver Miss Rees had left behind her, between the children and the young people.'

'Good Lord,' Tom said, 'I was sure there'd be something we'd forget. I remember now, that was the custom in Hendre Ddu when one of the older servants died without kith or kin. We'll have to remedy that. Tell Prosser that the youngsters must call here next Sunday after chapel.'

'But what about that first cousin from Tregaron?' Lowri said. 'Anyway, I wonder what money she will have left. She was very generous, you know, nobody from chapel ever got married or had a baby without her giving them a brand new crown, they could depend on that. And Christmas-time too, she used to get half a dozen pairs of woollen socks for all the men and stockings for the maids and always the best quality. Dear old Miss Rees. I really miss her. I don't think I ever realised how much I loved her.'

Tom admitted that he felt exactly the same. 'In a way we made fun of her loyalty to the family, but in fact we appreciated it and loved her for it.'

'Where's May?' Josi suddenly asked.

'She's up with Catrin and the baby. Catrin has been showing her all the old photographs. She's seen photos of you since you were a few days old,' she told Tom. 'Little Rachel May is going to be christened in her grandmother's old christening gown and bonnet and Catrin's asked May and me to be her godmothers.'

'I only hope the baby will put on a bit of weight before that,' Graham said, sighing like an old man, 'or she'll look like a little shrimp in all that magnificence of lace and tulle.'

'She'll be fine,' Josi said with more assurance than he really felt. 'What, lad, do you doubt that this thriving farming family with its history of breeding prize-winning stock is going to fail with one of their own? Not likely. I remember Tom here giving his mother a very anxious few weeks but look at him now.'

They all turned towards Tom who looked as strong and handsome as if he'd been on the continent doing the grand tour, not fighting in the mud and stinking slime of the trenches for two and a half years.

Three days later, May went back to London. On her last day at Hendre Ddu she seemed strangely dispirited and distant. Tom was worried, but comforted himself with the thought that she was dreading the time they would spend apart. Perhaps she expected her father to object to her sudden decision to get married and live so far away. He would quite understand it; if she were his daughter he'd feel exactly the same.

Chapter seven

It was Lowri who made the discovery. In the old press in Miss Rees' bedroom, under a pile of linen, was a brown canvas bag containing a great weight of gold sovereigns.

'Great Heavens,' Tom said when she took them to him. 'However did she manage to save this much money? Her wages were ridiculously small for all the work she did here. She always said that her status in the family was sufficient reward, but I was never convinced of that.'

'Shall I count it, Tom?' Lowri asked. 'I didn't want to touch it until I'd handed it over to you.'

'Let's do it together and try to decide what we'll do with it. I suppose she hasn't left any instructions or any sort of will?'

'No, I've been through all her papers. Though I'm afraid I've been unable to throw much away. It's all so interesting, accounts of how much Mrs Ifans spent on her wedding outfit when she married your father, stuff like that. How much was spent on the Harvest Festival supper and at Christmas and the New Year festivities. We should keep it all together in a big cardboard box. It would make a history of the house since she first came here at fourteen, over sixty years ago. About 1854 I think it was, not long after Mrs Ifans' mother died. And as well as that, as the minister said, she had gleaned information about the Morgan family over generations and had taken the trouble to write it all down in her lovely copperplate handwriting.'

But Tom seemed unable to think of anything but the money. 'Let's put them in piles of ten and add them up. I'm beginning to realise what joy misers have in counting up their gold, doesn't it give you some sort of a deeply sensuous pleasure? I'm afraid it does me.'

'Well, it's in your family, they say, that miser strain. Your great-grandfather now, he was a hard, grasping man according to what I've heard.' It was the first time Lowri had dared tease Tom, as Josi and Catrin always did.

'And don't I know it! It was that man who took my father's inheritance, Cefn Hebog, to pay off some paltry debt. He's never let me forget that. Hasn't he ever told you about it?'

'No. He must have forgiven him now that you've righted old wrongs and given it back to him. He loves Cefn Hebog and so do I.'

'When May and I are married and we've got a farm manager here, you might be able to go back there. Though I shall dread the day. I think families should stick together. I even love having Catrin and the baby back here.'

'Have you noticed anything about the dates of these sovereigns?' Lowri asked him after a few moments.

'No, should I have?'

'They're all quite old. I mean, all of them have Victoria's head on them. When did her son, Edward, come to the throne?'

'In 1902 or 1903. I know Catrin and I are both Victorian babies and so are you probably.'

'Yes, I'm six months older than Miss Catrin, Catrin I mean.'

'When did my grandfather die? I was about four years old then. Catrin doesn't even remember him. But you're quite right, none of these is from the new century. Perhaps she got all of them from my grandfather, they all seem from the time he was alive. Great Heavens, I wonder whether Miss Rees was his mistress. It would explain why she never got married. She used to tell us about all the rich widowers who'd courted her. She used to say that it was Mother she couldn't leave, but there might have been another reason.'

'Oh Tom, Miss Rees has only been dead a week and you're already blackening her character.'

'Not at all. Why shouldn't they both have had some pleasure in life, they both worked hard enough. Anyway, it was you who noticed that they were all old, what were you thinking about when you mentioned that? It's certainly intriguing. I think we've got about five hundred sovereigns here all told. Whatever shall we do with it all?'

'You could take May to London for your honeymoon and stay in a grand hotel with great gold bathrooms and carpets everywhere and live a life of luxury for six months or more.'

'I'll tell you one thing. That first cousin from Tregaron is not going to have a penny of it. She never visited Miss Rees in all the years I remember, though Miss Rees was always so proud of her. She was a schoolmistress and later married a sea captain from New Quay and had "visited the heathen lands across the sea".'

'She'll have plenty of money then. Sea captains have always been rich.'

'Is that my father coming in? Tell him I want to see him please, Lowri. What's he going to think of this little lot?'

Josi had plenty to say. 'I don't know how she came by it and I don't much care. But I know what you should do with it. You should make Davy Prosser your manager and build him a decent house with some modern facilities. Brithdir is all but falling down, but naturally the man just tries to patch it up instead of complaining about it. Speak to him about it this very afternoon.'

'That's a good suggestion. Just as long as no one else has any claim on it. Perhaps we should wait a few days in case something else turns up amongst her papers.'

'No, I think I've been through pretty well everything now,' Lowri said. 'But anyway, you can surely have a house built on your own land for a fraction of that money.'

'I think Tom's loath to part with his little haul,' she told her husband.

'I wouldn't be surprised. That's the Morgan blood coming out in him. Did I ever tell you about old Thomas Morgan, the one he was named after? He was a noted money-lender and thief. What he used to do was offer to lend a little struggling smallholder fifty pounds or so when his harvest had failed on the understanding that he would pay it back in a year's time. Of course the man would take it. What other option did he have? And that's how he'd lose his little farm. How do I know? Because that's what happened to my grandfather, old Amos Evans, that's how he lost Cefn Hebog that had been in his family for three hundred years.'

'How many times have you told me that story? What would it take to shut you up once and for all? I thought giving you back Cefn Hebog might do it, but no. You're a pitiless, unforgiving wretch.'

'Apologise to your son,' Lowri said, 'And make it up, I beg you.'

'We're friends really, don't worry. I like to tease him a bit, that's all. I don't want him to forget that he's got bad blood in him.'

'I'll put this money back in Miss Rees' room then until you decide what to do with it,' Lowri said. 'We don't want Tom to get too fond of it,' she added.

That night, Tom had another nightmare, but this time when his father had rushed to his bedroom he cried and talked for a short while. About treading on blackened corpses in the slime of the trenches. 'So many dead,' he moaned, 'so many arms and legs, so many mutilated faces.'

'You must work towards a lasting peace, my son,' Josi murmured tenderly. 'It's being called the war to end all wars. You must see to it that it is. Make that your life's work.

What could be more worthwhile? You've got the energy and the means. You must work to stop the killing. Work for world peace.' Josi went on repeating the same sentences until he hardly knew what he was saying, and Tom fell asleep again, still holding on to his hand. And Josi sat at his side until morning.

On Monday morning Tom was surprised and disappointed that there was no letter from May. 'Do you think her father has forbidden her to marry me?'

'Of course not,' Josi said. 'Why should he? And you a soldier and, he probably thinks, a gentleman. And he must have heard something about you two. After all, she's been writing to you for nearly three years and all that time you've been writing back to her. He can't have been unaware of all those army letters reaching her from France. She's probably got a lot of people to see and hasn't had too much time for letter writing. You'll hear from her by the end of the week I'm sure.'

Josi was wrong. Tom heard nothing at all from his fiancée until the Monday of the following week and that letter brought heart-rending news. May was very sorry but felt she'd promised to marry him without sufficient consideration. Now that she'd given the matter further thought she'd decided that she didn't know him well enough to commit to being his wife and would be pleased if he would be good enough to free her from her too-hasty engagement. She hoped that they could remain friends and that he would still write to her from time to time.

Tom was completely devastated. 'What happened to her?' he asked his father and Lowri. 'I can't take this rejection, can't make any sense of it. When she left here everything was fine. All I had to worry about was her journey back to London, the trains being so badly affected by the war.'

'I'm not so sure that she was absolutely happy even on that Friday morning,' Lowri said at last. 'I felt she was worried about something. I asked her how she was feeling, expecting her to say she was excited about telling her father or something of that sort, but all she said was that she would always remember us. I felt it was an odd thing to say, but put it down to the fact that she was so sad to be leaving Tom even for a week or two. What's at the back of this change of heart? I feel really disappointed in her. Unless there's some explanation we haven't thought about.'

'There is a very obvious explanation. Look at me. I'm a wreck.'

'You're a war hero,' Josi said. 'And even Mari Elen thinks you're as handsome as a prince. She wondered last night whether you would marry her if you were free. I said I thought you would.'

'And May wouldn't have fallen in love with you if she thought you were a wreck. And she certainly did fall in love with you, Tom. I saw Catrin and Edward years ago, I saw your father with Miriam. I know the face of love.'

'Josi,' Lowri suddenly added. 'I'm going to go up to London to find out why she's changed her mind. I'm not going to let Tom lose her without a fight. I shall make her tell me what it is that's worrying her.'

'Great heavens, Lowri, what a little fighter I married. Just look at her, Tom. I'm terrified of her.... Are you sure you feel up to it, cariad? You've never been to London.'

One look at her face gave him the answer. 'So when will you go, my love?' he asked meekly.

'On the first train tomorrow morning. No, I've never been to London, so I don't want to arrive late in the evening.'

'But how will you find your way about? I'd have no idea how to set about it. She told me that she and her father lived in St John's Wood. What part of London is that? I'd never heard of it.'

'Tom will give me her address and I'll take a taxi from Paddington. It'll probably cost a lot of money, but someone has to speak to her. I'm not having Tom trying to work out what happened and probably blaming himself for something that isn't his fault.'

'Lowri, I'll always remember this,' Tom said. 'If I wasn't so incapacitated I'd be going myself.'

'Well, I'm your step-mother now, don't forget. You two look after Catrin and Mari Elen and leave May to me.'

'But do you have any London clothes and a suitcase and so on?'

'Oh, I shan't stay long, one night at the most, and my chapel clothes are surely good enough for a day trip to London. I have my wedding hat too, don't forget. Everyone said I looked a proper toff in that. You needn't feel ashamed of me.'

'As though we would,' Tom said. 'It's proud of you we feel.'

'I'm speechless,' was all Josi could say. 'Absolutely speechless.'

'But I want to come with you,' Mari Elen sobbed the next morning. 'I've never been on a train in my whole life.'

'We'll go to the seaside by train before the end of the summer,' Lowri promised her. She would have promised anything to escape the little girl's hot, clutching hands.

'But I want to come to London with you today. I want to visit my Auntie May and go to the zoo and see an elephant. I've already been to the seaside and I don't like all that sand in my knickers and I don't much like the sea, anyway, it's too sudden and too splashy. And how do I know you're ever coming back, even?'

'I'll be back tomorrow, probably before you go to bed. And if you promise to be a very good girl for your daddy, I'll bring you a new doll.'

'With yellow hair and blue eyes that open and shut like a real baby?'

'Yes.'

'And a white shawl all pretty holes like baby Rachel's?'

'Certainly.'

'All right, I suppose.' Heavy sigh and long sniff. 'I don't want you to go but I hope you have a nice time. Have you got a hankie and some mints?'

'Goodbye, cariad. No, you must let go of me now or I'll miss the train.'

Lowri managed to pull herself free and hurried out to the motor car where Graham was waiting to take her to the station.

'I had a long talk with Catrin,' he told her as soon as she was settled by his side. 'I think she felt much better when I told her how I'd felt when my first wife, Angela, died. I told her over and over again how I'd suffered and how I'd never dreamed I would ever love again. And I insisted that though my love for her was a different sort of love, less passionate perhaps, it was still very deep and true. And eventually she accepted what I said and thought it might be similar to how she felt about me.'

'I'm so glad. You both deserve some happiness. How long ago was it that your first wife died?'

'Almost four years ago. It will be four years in September.'

'It's almost three years now since Miriam died. You know about Miriam don't you?'

'Yes, poor thing. And I think a suicide is more difficult to get over than any other type of death, even a death in battle. It seems such a betrayal somehow, such a failure of love.'

'Yes. Poor Josi. I think he is still tormented by that. Graham, why do you think May has broken off her engagement to Tom? Have you any thoughts about that?'

'Perhaps, looking back on her stay with us, she found us altogether too wild and strange. It took me quite a long time to get used to the Welsh and the Welsh way of life. And I was Scottish, a nearer clan altogether. The English are very unemotional and insular, I've found. Anyway, I'm glad you're going to try to find out something else from her. Things really understood are easier to accept. Anyway, you're a dear good girl and a great support to us all. Catrin loves you as a sister, I know that and I've always been very fond of you. Here we are. Now, take good care of yourself.'

On the way up to London, Lowri tried to work out a possible reason for May's failure of nerve, and try as she might she still feared that it was something to do with her, possibly her low status in the family. It was that unease that had made her determined to travel to London.

She had a hot, tedious journey, with a very long delay at Oxford, and didn't arrive at Paddington until six that evening. By that time, she was full of worries and doubts. Whatever is May going to think when I arrive at their house? What if she doesn't invite me to spend the night? Where shall I go? Will she tell me where to find a small inexpensive hotel? Have I got enough money? Hotels in London are hideously expensive, I know that. Oh, I wish I was at home in Cefn Hebog.

Chapter eight

At last baby Rachel seemed to have got the hang of sucking and Catrin was feeling far more relaxed. From the blackness that had engulfed her she emerged smiling wanly, ready to wonder at May's defection and at Lowri's bravery in travelling to London to tackle her.

'Look, Tom, look at her little blue eyelids, she's really quite pretty, isn't she, when she's asleep and not crying, look at the curl of her lips, look at those perfect little fingernails. And now, look, she's frowning in her sleep. Oh, Sidan bach. That was what Nano used to call me. Tom, you do love her, don't you?'

'Of course I do. I wish you'd stay here for a few months at least, so that I can really get to know her. A child's uncle, her mother's brother, was his closest relative in ancient Welsh culture. The identity of the father might well be unknown so the mother's eldest brother took over his responsibilities.'

There was a long silence while they both gazed at the baby.

'Were you as surprised as I was about that letter from May?' Tom eventually asked her.

'Of course I was. Graham and I spent ages trying to think of a rational explanation.'

'But these things are never rational, are they? Falling in love is never rational. As soon as I met May I just seemed to be struck with the awareness that she and I belonged together. I never gave it any thought. It was as simple as that. A thunderbolt. I know some men try to start a relationship before being sent abroad simply because they want someone to write to them but I didn't even have to ask May to write. I took it for granted that she would.'

'And she seemed so ready to become part of the family,' Catrin said. 'We were so happy for you. What could have upset her?'

'She must have decided she couldn't marry a man who's lost a leg and is also subject to terrifying nightmares. It's not altogether surprising, is it?'

'Yes it is. Having seen you two together, I find it completely surprising.... Oh, Tom, she's waking up. Oh, heavens, she's going to start crying again. Oh, just listen to her. She's been fed and bathed and changed, what can she want now? Oh Tom, please help me. Oh, if only Lowri was here. Or Nano. They knew exactly what to do with Mari Elen.'

The tiny baby's pathetic little bleats, laa-laa-laaa, seemed to fill the whole room, the whole world.

'What about your little nursemaid?'

'Molly? She was up for such a long time last night, I made her go to bed for a rest.'

'Babies do cry; you just have to accept it. If only I could march about with her over my shoulder – babies like that. But I'm good for nothing.'

'Please don't start to feel sorry for yourself. You've been so wonderful.'

'We'll send for Mrs Prosser. Ring the bell for Maud, she'll fetch her in no time.'

'That's a good idea, Tom. Oh, I feel so hopeless.'

'Well, you're a very new mother… but please don't start feeling sorry for youself,' he added pointedly.

'Maud, could you please go over to ask Mrs Prosser to come here as soon as she can. We can't seem to stop this little thing crying.'

'Let me take her to the kitchen, Mister Tom. I think she'd like to be swaddled tight in a shawl. I know it's very warm, Miss Catrin, but small babies always seem to feel safer wrapped in a shawl. Let me do it. I'll walk about with her. What a dear little doll she is. She's very like you, Miss Catrin.'

'My goodness, you've quietened her,' Tom said. 'Maud, how do you know so much about babies?'

'I've got seven younger brothers and sisters, Mister Tom, the latest not so much older than this one.'

'Maud, will please you ask Mrs Hopkins whether she can spare you to look after baby Rachel this morning? I've sent Molly to have a little rest because she was up such a lot in the night.'

'She'll get used to it, Miss Catrin. I have.'

'How old are you, Maud?'

'Turned seventeen now, Mr Tom.'

'And you must find the work here very hard?'

'Oh no. This is a good place, Hendre Ddu, everybody knows that. We have comfortable, shop-bought beds and as much food as we want. I wouldn't be anywhere else.'

'You're a good girl, Maud.'

Catrin and Tom were both exhausted after their five-minute ordeal with the baby. Now that she was quiet and in another room, nothing else seemed to matter quite as much.

'Seven children as well as Maud,' Catrin murmured at last. 'I'm definitely only having one.'

'Things will seem very different in a few years,' Tom said.

'I wonder whether things will come right for me,' he added afterwards. 'I don't think so. It seemed too good to be true.'

'May was lovely but no better than you deserve. You've been through so much.'

'You've been through quite a lot yourself, haven't you, one way or another? How could I have been so blind? I had no idea you and Edward cared for each other.'

Catrin stared at him:

Mae'r esgyd fach yn gwasgu,
Mewn man nas gwyddoch chi.

Do you remember that song? I sang it – unaccompanied – in the school eisteddfod one year. Won first prize, too. Poor

Edward and poor Rose. She lost him too. I wonder how she is? I'd like to meet her. I've had two or three letters from her.'

'Did she ever find out about Edward's feelings for you?'

'Yes. He wanted to make a clean breast of everything before that last battle. I think he had a premonition that he was going to be killed.'

'So many of us were, especially in that first year, that first big offensive at Ypres. Everything that could go wrong, did. There was so much quite unbelievable incompetence. Oh, I'm lucky to be alive and out of it.'

'I'm so glad you're back here safe and sound,' Catrin said. 'I'm so fond of you, Tom. I never used to be, but I am now.' She put her hand on his arm.

When Josi and Mari Elen came back from their morning at Cefn Hebog they found Catrin much calmer and the baby fast asleep. To their surprise, Mari Elen had also chosen to have a nap on the sofa, a thing she hadn't done for months.

'She's been very active, fair play,' Josi said, 'but I think she also doesn't like not being the centre of attraction and wants to be a baby again. Tom was the same. When you were born, he even started to wet the bed again, I remember.'

'Well, thanks for that,' Tom said.

'You know I've been thinking a lot about Nano,' Catrin said quickly. 'I'm not really happy with your explanation of that money she had. Yes, maybe she had some affair with our grandfather, but I can't believe she took money from him. That would have made her what she would have called "a wicked woman". Like the ones in the Bible. You know, "She lieth in wait for him at every corner and sayeth unto him, Come, I have peace offerings with me."'

'Is that in the Bible?' Josi asked. 'I don't think we have that in the Welsh version or I'd have found it as a boy. We lads used to spend a lot of time in Sunday school searching for the interesting bits.... It was educational,' he added.

'I tend to agree with you, Catrin,' Tom said. 'I was thinking along the same lines myself when I was lying awake last night and trying not to think about May. But I can't come up with any other explanation. Not for five hundred pounds.'

'Unless he left it to her in his will. Because she'd turned down offers of marriage, for instance, and chosen to stay with Mother when she was very young. He might have wanted to repay her loyalty.'

'But five hundred sovereigns would have been excessive,' Josi said. 'He was his father's son, after all. Not an out-and-out tyrannical miser like old Thomas Morgan I grant you, but a miserable old fellow all the same. Trust me, I know. I had plenty of dealings with him. Fifty pounds in his will I could just about believe in, but not five hundred. Never.'

'And when I got into debt in Oxford that time, I can't believe that Nano wouldn't have let me have twenty sovereigns if she had all that.'

'But she might have considered that spoiling you. She was very keen on teaching us right and proper principles, wasn't she? I'm going to look through her papers again. Lowri put them all together, so you can help me, Tom, this afternoon.'

'It will help pass the time, I suppose,' he said, without much enthusiasm. 'I wonder when we can expect Lowri back?'

'I'm very anxious about her,' Josi said, 'don't you start. She's never been further than Carmarthen before, and she didn't enjoy that. She's like me, not happy unless she has fields and trees around her.'

After dinner – and Mari Elen had brought herself to the table as soon as she'd heard the sound of cutlery – and when the baby had had another long but fairly successful feed, Catrin went up to Miss Rees' bedroom and brought down the large cardboard box Lowri had filled with her mementoes: drawings, letters and cards. Finding the drawings, all by Catrin or Tom at various stages, was like coming across an old diary of their lives; they could remember the occasions they had been asked to record: a new puppy, a new pony, a birthday party, a snow storm, Christmas and New Year's Day. In some of the old letters the writing was faded and yellow, but most of them were just about decipherable. There were long letters from their mother 'to my beloved Nano' whenever she was on holiday and later when she was at boarding school in Malvern and very homesick. They were all highly interesting to her children, but they came across nothing referring in any way to the mysterious money.

Though Molly had got up before dinner, so that Catrin could feel quite easy about the baby, they both felt too tired to finish the whole collection.

'We've done very well, we'll be able to finish tomorrow afternoon. We've gone through well over half.'

'Yes. And I think I should practise some walking now. I'll get Father to come with me for twenty minutes or so. It will be wonderful to be out in this weather. Don't you feel up to a spot of fresh air? I used to dream of Hendre Ddu air when I was in France: healthy air and farm smells, hay and cows. Instead, there was always the stink of sweaty feet and rotting bodies in the slime of the trenches, the wounded and the dying and of course the still-unburied dead outside.'

'How could anyone survive and remain even relatively sane?' Catrin asked.

For a long time they sat in silence, the walk forgotten.

Chapter nine

Catrin had asked Graham to meet the two trains arriving from London, one at four-fifteen and one at seven-fifty. It was soon apparent that Lowri hadn't caught the earlier one; was that good or bad, Catrin wondered.

But they both arrived in time for a late supper. Lowri looked tired, of course, but she had obviously not received any very encouraging news. She looked pleased to be back with them, but not happy.

'Please tell us now,' Tom said. 'We're all in this together and I can't wait for that quiet moment when we're alone.'

'It's very much as you suspected, Tom. She's simply afraid that she was swept away with the happiness of seeing you again so that she made an over-hasty decision, over-hasty, she said, I remember those words, not the wrong decision. She said she loved your house and your family and so on, but when she left here, it all seemed like a dream rather than real life. She said that even before she'd arrived home she'd started to have these doubts and that what her father thought about it had only strengthened them.

Something like that. She talked for hours. I was exhausted but we didn't go to bed until almost midnight. But she seemed really pleased to see me so that she could try to explain herself.'

Catrin was the first to speak. 'That sounds much more hopeful than her letter. You must write to her, Tom, and tell her you understand exactly how she feels and will be prepared to wait.'

'That's all you can do, son,' Josi said. 'And if I was a betting man, and luckily that's one of the sins that's never tormented me, I'd be willing to put a tidy sum of money on the fact that she'll come round. Women can't resist the thought that someone truly loves them… and quite right too, it doesn't happen too often in anybody's lifetime,' he added lamely.

'I don't know about that,' Graham said. 'Do you remember "Gather ye rosebuds while ye may"? Some little poem from schooldays. Something by Robbie Burns probably.'

'I'm not talking about gathering roses,' his father-in-law replied sourly. 'Though I did enough of that, I'm afraid. I'm talking about that love that, that, oh, I'm no poet, but you must understand what I mean.'

'It's not Robbie Burns anyway,' Tom said, 'it's Herrick. And now Lowri, listen to me, I don't want to see you in the kitchen tomorrow. You sit in the parlwr with Catrin all day. Now that's an order.'

Catrin felt pleased at the change of subject. 'Still giving orders, then?' she asked.

Tom smiled and they all relaxed.

'Now try to tell your old fellow exactly why you were ready to step into the lion's den as you did,' Josi asked Lowri when they were in their bedroom later. 'You didn't try to see that old fool Lloyd George as well, did you? While you were up there? I won't put anything past you from now on.'

'Don't be silly. I was nervous, I admit that, and I wouldn't have dared do it except that I was worried that it was all something to do with me.'

'With you? What can you mean? Do you mean because you were once a servant? Nonsense. The big nobs all marry chorus girls, it's a well known fact. Lords and earls and so on.'

'Yes, I'm sure you know a lot about these lords and earls. No, you see, I saw my sister, Sali, talking away to her when she'd gone into the kitchen on the day of the funeral.'

'And?'

'When she was about fourteen and a maid here, Tom made her fall in love with him. Oh, I know it wasn't intentional or anything like that. But he was so especially kind to her. Because she'd been crying over something, I think. And you know how foolish girls can be at that age. She imagined she was madly in love with him and started to make a big romance out of it. I never knew it at the time, my mother never mentioned it, but I'm sure now that that's why Miss Rees asked Mother to take her away. She must have been saying things to the other maids, I heard that Miss Rees didn't even give her any sort of reference.'

'She could be very harsh. She was to me. But what could Sali, silly girl or not, have told her that was so very bad?'

'I mentioned seeing them talking in the kitchen to May,

but she wouldn't tell me much and I don't want to repeat what she did say because I think it might concern you, too.'

'As though I care about that. You won't tell me? Look, I'm going to tickle you in that particularly ticklish spot near your left armpit until you do.'

'Oh, stop, stop! I will tell you, I will, I promise.... Well I rather thought it was something to do with Mari Elen, I mean that she was not mine, but a... oh, I can't even bring myself to say it.'

'You mean that she was a hedge-child? I honestly can't believe that such a thing as that could have caused her to make such a huge decision. Upper class people don't seem to care about those little details, anyway.'

'Oh, don't start again about those dukes and earls. Where do you read such rubbish?'

'Certainly not in the Good Book, as Miss Rees would say.'

They fell asleep.

Mrs Prosser called next day to tell them that one of her daughters had won a scholarship to the grammar school, the only one in her year. Tom was very proud of her, he was her godfather, and promised to get her a bike so that she could ride back and fore to school. They also told her what Miss Rees had told Catrin, that she was to have her three or four books. 'We need to contact her cousin from Tregaron,' Tom added. 'She is to have her dresses, I believe. I'm surprised she didn't turn up for the funeral. We had the notice in *The Tivyside* and in the *Western Mail*. Strange that no one let her know. Perhaps she's not well herself. She could be dead as far as we know. Miss Rees never heard from her, I know that much.'

'She did leave a will, then, did she?' Mrs Prosser asked.

'No. We found nothing written down. We only know some of her wishes because she had a word with Catrin when she was taken ill. It would be good if we had more exact knowledge of her wishes.'

'You've looked in her Bible, Mister Tom?'

'No. What makes you think it would be there?'

'That's where old people used to leave their wills long ago. A sheet of paper it would be, like as not. Nothing official, no legal obligation, only what they wished. In the Book of Proverbs it would be. That chapter about money being the root of all evil. Mr Isaacs often preached about that.'

'Money being the root of all evil?'

'Only that isn't what it says in the Bible, that was his point. It's the love of money is the root of all evil, that was his point. Money was neither good nor bad in itself. It was to be respected and not wasted on drink or gambling or… you know that word about wicked women. It was the love of money that was evil. Those people who have plenty for themselves and wouldn't pay a penny for anyone even if they might be starving. That was his point. You look in that page, Mister Tom. I can't tell you chapter and verse but Proverbs is only a short book anyway.'

'We will, Mrs Prosser. Thank you very much. We'll tell you what we discover next time you call. Now, you tell Gwenllian to call here to tell me what bike she'd like.

Perhaps the best thing would be for Lowri here to take her down to town and she can make her choice. Could you manage that, Lowri?'

'Yes of course. Next Saturday morning tell her that we'll go in on the ten o'clock bus.'

'Thank you very much. You're too good to us.' Mrs Prosser left wiping her eyes on the bottom of her apron.

'Oh, God,' Tom said, 'I feel so guilty.'

He went to Miss Rees' bedroom, but there was no sign of her Bible. 'You've never been able to find anything,' Catrin said. 'I'll go as soon as I've got baby Rachel out of her bath.'

It was Lowri who finally found the Bible and the sheet of paper Mrs Prosser had predicted. It was begun in legal terms, 'I, Hannah Rees being of sound mind etc,' but very soon slipped into her ordinary voice. 'Now, I'm not going to bother you with the small and unimportant brooches and necklaces I leave behind. I only leave one thing of note. Five hundred sovereigns in a brown canvas bag hidden under my clothes and stockings in the oak cwpwrdd tridarn in my bedroom. I know Mr Ifans won't like hearing about this, but I have to explain it. The night before Miss Rachel got married, this bag was handed over to me by her father, old Griff Morgan. He explained to me that after Rachel's marriage all her worldly goods, all he would leave her, would become her husband's. He wanted to make sure that if any time he might desert her, she would have that five hundred sovereigns which were in my possession. You did desert her, Mr Ifans, but because you were a good man, you didn't take anything of hers with you so there never seemed any point in telling Mrs Ifans that her father had provided for just such an occasion. It has long been a worry to me, and I would like the money to go to Hendre Ddu, to Mister Tom, as soon as he's able to take up the reins again. I know he will want to make improvements, I heard him tell his father that he wanted to change things and all this will take money. That Mister Tom may come home safely and use it wisely is the only wish of his old nurse and I'm sure his mother too. Signed Hannah Theodosia Rees October 25th 1914.'

Everyone in the room was on the point of tears as Catrin read out the will.

'What a good and honourable woman she was,' Josi said. 'She even had the grace to forgive me, I think, though I behaved so badly.'

'But you came back to Mother, Tada,' Catrin cried. 'Of course she forgave you. We all did.'

'We all did,' Tom echoed. 'You gave up everything and paid the price.'

Josi thought of the price he had paid and sighed. Lowri noticed that he started to hum the same old song that he always hummed when he was thinking of Miriam. She managed to smile at him and he smiled back at her, a brave, watery smile with tears in it.

Dinner was very late that day. Mari Elen came in complaining long and hard. 'Things are not so good around here any more. That old baby in everybody's way and it's rice pudding again instead of raspberry tart though I asked for it last night. When can we go back to Cefn

Hebog? Cefn Hebog is best, isn't it Dada?'

'Yes I think it is. But all the same, this is where I'd rather be at the moment, raspberry tart or no. This is our family; your step-mother, your father, your sister and your brother.'

'When shall I have a baby sister? Maudie said it won't be long now. What do you think?'

'Maudie's got seven brothers and sisters. I don't think we'd have enough room for seven, do you?'

'Definitely not. Just one more and one more kitten. That would make me happy. Maudie has only got a tin roof on her house and the rain comes in. She wants her sister, Betty, to work in Hendre Ddu when she leaves school. Can she? Because Maudie is going to leave at Christmas to get married. Only it's a secret and oh, I wish I hadn't told you. I promised her I wouldn't tell you.'

'But she's only about seventeen, Maud, or did she say eighteen?' Tom said. 'Why does she want to get married so young?'

'Perhaps Maudie's family can have Prosser's house when we build him a new one. At least it's got a good slate roof. And Maud's father is a builder's mate, I think. He might be able to do some repairs to the old place. That's another secret, mind. It may not come about so don't say a word to Maud at present. Promise?'

'I promise. Can I go to Sunday School with her tomorrow?'

It was a couple of days later that Lowri received a letter – which turned out to be from May. May thanked her for taking the trouble to come to London to see her and wished she might come again for a longer stay.

So much was expected; the second part of the letter was a thunderbolt. Lowri was pleased that she was by herself when she read it so that she could compose herself before showing it to Tom and Josi. This is what May wrote:

> *Tom and I told each other our secrets. I told him that I hadn't had a previous boyfriend, he told me that he hadn't had a girlfriend. And I believed him. If he had trusted me with his secret I think I could have forgiven him, in fact I'm certain of it. But I feel I can't forgive that he told me an out-and-out lie, leaving it to poor Sali to break my heart. She, poor thing, told me about their affair when she was only fifteen and how Mari Elen was their child who had been taken away from her and given to Mr Evans and yourself to bring up. Her eyes were full of tears as she revealed this to me and she made me promise not to tell Tom, because she'd promised him that she never would. But oh, Lowri, her eyes when she told me! I could hardly bring myself to be civil to Tom afterwards and only longed to be on the train and alone with my grief. Oh, Lowri, I loved him so much. And you couldn't believe how I could let him down. Dear Lowri, I feel I owe it to you to explain myself even though it's betraying little Sali's trust. Please try to forgive me. You may show this letter to Tom if you feel it would help him understand my 'cruelty'.*

Yes Lowri, that's what you accused me of. Please believe that I would have loved to be part of your wonderful family.
Ever yours, May.

Lowri sent Maud to the clos with a note for Josi. 'Josi, I need you. Please come at once whatever you're doing.'

He came at once. 'Whatever's the matter with you? Lowri, you're white as a potato. Sit down this minute.'

She sat down and passed him the letter. 'Oh, Josi, I'm glad to have you to turn to,' she said. He said nothing for a long time.

'Well,' he said at last. 'It's good news really because it shows that May hasn't changed her mind, but has been deceived. You shall show the letter to Tom and I shall go to fetch Sali and bring her back here with me and here she shall stay until May comes back. Then she shall confess her lies to May and we'll all put it behind us and forget all about it. Take this to Tom.'

'Don't frighten Sali. I think she's suffering from some mental trouble. My mother was talking to Mr Isaacs about her one Sunday and he advised her to take her to see Dr Rhys Vaughan and she said she would as soon as they can afford his prices.'

'I won't frighten her, merch-i. It's the truth we're looking for not revenge. She's my sister-in-law remember and I'm quite fond of the daft little creature.'

Tom wrote to May. The letter took him a great deal of effort and time. Several times he left it and they heard him walking about. His leg was giving him a great deal of discomfort as though it was suffering with him. At last the letter was ready and Josi, not prepared to trust the little post box in the village, cycled to put it in the post office in town.

Sali was in the house and had been given a bed in Maud and Lottie's room. Maud said she was crying a great deal, but wouldn't accept that she had lied to May.

'Does she really believe this story she's invented? Is she sane, say?' Catrin asked. 'We're not going to punish her. She knows that all we ask is that she tells May that she never had an affair with Tom and that she isn't Mari Elen's mother.'

'I'll have to tell Sali about Miriam,' Lowri said. 'I think we probably made it too much of a secret and she was too young to understand the truth. She'll remember Miriam because she was her teacher and I remember she cried when she left school. She's old enough now to understand these things. I'll take her some tea and talk to her, make her understand how wrong she's been.'

Sali seemed to cry less after Lowri's talk and she started to help Maud round the house.

Tom's letter must have had the right effect because May promised to come again on the Friday on the same train as she had before. It was to be their second chance. She agreed not to break off their engagement. They would be married in the spring of next year, February was her birthday month. Would Tom have any objections to a small February wedding?

Tom, walking about like a man in a trance, seemed to have no objections

Chapter ten

This time Lowri had a wonderful meal ready for May. It seemed to everyone a pre-celebration of the wedding to come. Sali was brought in and though she wasn't prepared to say she had lied, she did manage to say that she was sorry to have given offence. It wasn't enough for Graham Andrews. 'All right,' he said, 'if you are the mother then how was it that I brought Mari Elen into the world just over four years ago and to a Miriam Lewis, spinster of this parish. If I were to examine you, Sali, I feel sure that I would find you a virgin. Are you trying to tell us that you are the second virgin mother? And that Mari Elen is some sort of freak? Tell us. You have been a very wicked girl and I think you are being dealt with too kindly.'

'That's enough, Graham,' Josi said, suddenly head of the family. 'I want you to remember, please, that she is my wife's sister and related to all of us. You may go now, Sali. We all think you've been very foolish but not wicked. You and the other girls can finish off the sherry trifle between you as long as you remember to leave a portion for Mari Elen's breakfast.'

'Is she all right, Lowri?' he asked his wife. 'Go and see that she's not crying, will you love?'

'Very, very wicked girl,' was all Graham would say, so that at last Catrin lost her temper and said, quite kindly, 'Oh shut up you silly old fool. Stop trying to behave like your terrible old ancestors.'

He smiled at that, only complaining that he could have done with a second helping of the trifle.

The next day was full of sunshine. The week had been cold and rainy, but that Saturday was glorious. Lowri went off to town with Gwenllian to buy her the best possible bike: 'a good strong one allowing for growth and made for riding five miles to school every day, good brakes and three gears. Pretend to let Gwenllian choose but guide her choice.'

'Right,' Lowri said, 'leave it to me. We'll be home on the ten past twelve.'

If Lowri had not been in town, she might have noticed Mari Elen's disappearance much earlier. As it was, it was nearly one o'clock before she suddenly said, 'Where's the child? Where's Mari Elen?'

Tom was sure he'd seen her with her father. 'She was here when we had coffee wasn't she?'

'No,' May said, 'I haven't seen her since breakfast when she had a boiled egg followed by a big helping of trifle. She hasn't been in since then. She wasn't with Josi when he came in for dinner.

'No, I haven't seen her all morning,' he said when asked.

They sent to Mrs Prosser to ask whether Mari Elen

been there playing with Rhian, but Mrs Prosser hadn't seen her that morning.

'Is Sali here?' Lowri asked Maud, who was carrying in the dinner.

'No, she went back home this morning.'

'She surely didn't take Mari Elen with her?' Lowri asked, suddenly feeling frightened.

For once, Graham arrived at the right time for a meal, but he wasn't allowed to sit. 'Graham dear, you must go out at once to look for Mari Elen. We're afraid that Sali might have taken Mari Elen with her. I don't know where they went. Try their house first. Lowri, perhaps you ought to go with him.'

'I'll go with him,' Josi said. 'Lowri, don't worry. We'll have her back in no time. They can't have gone far.'

Sali's mother hadn't seen her. She hadn't known how long they wanted her daughter to stay at Hendre Ddu, so she didn't know when to expect her. Was she in trouble?'

'No. We think she's got Mari Elen with her, that's all, and we want to make sure they're safe.'

The mother promised to send word to them as soon as they turned up. Josi felt frightened because she was so obviously worried. No word came all afternoon. Everyone became very worried. How much money did Sali have? Her mother wasn't sure. Sali wasn't working at the moment but she had certainly had some money for helping on the day of the funeral. She had given her nothing.

'Mari Elen has some money,' Lowri said. 'I don't know how much. She keeps it an old toffee tin in her room. I'll go to see if it's still there. It's only coppers, of course.'

It wasn't, there was not a penny left in the old tin. The two must have decided to go somewhere. Maud and Lottie were asked if they'd heard the girls discussing any plans, but they hadn't. They could only say that Sali seemed to have some sort of power over Mari Elen. Mari Elen seemed rather frightened of her, Maud thought. Both girls were given leave to search all the farm buildings and Josi said the person to find the girls would be given a substantial reward. The young servant lad was offered the same. 'Any sighting, any news. Ask everyone you see. Leave no stone unturned.'

It was the gwas bach, Hywel, who brought them the first news. He'd had the good sense to cycle to the station to ask if anyone there remembered seeing a small girl and her nursemaid on the platform and a porter had scratched his head and said, yes, he'd seen them. They were off somewhere from the other platform. He'd remembered seeing them crossing the bridge. They looked very excited, he remembered that, as though they were off to the seaside for the day. No, there was no bucket and spade, but the child was carrying a toy rabbit or a teddy bear, he remembered that too. The ticket office was closed and wouldn't be open until the following morning at seven. When had the girls been seen? It was before nine o'clock that morning.

Hywel was thanked and praised for his initiative. He was given half a crown and a slice of fruit cake for his reward.

'They'll come back this evening, won't they?' Catrin asked in a shaky voice. 'They won't dare stay out overnight.'

They sat and waited, getting more and more worried. Graham was dispatched to the station to meet every train arriving that evening. He came back after the last train had arrived.

Josi spoke. 'Tomorrow we'll have to contact the police. Perhaps we ought to do it tonight. If they're out roaming the streets they would be more visible late at night, Where did they go?'

Sali's mother sent word to say that the Sunday School trip was to Aberystwyth the previous year and that Sali had loved the town and had talked of it ever since. Was there a train to Aberystwyth at the time they'd been spotted in the station?

'I'll take you to Aberystwyth, Josi,' Graham said. 'We're not going to get any sleep if we do nothing. Let's go. The police there may have some news.'

But there was none. There'd been no report of anyone who seemed lost. The policeman on duty promised to send word if there should be any sighting the next day.

There was absolutely nothing they could do but wait for news. Sunday seemed endless. The strain was telling on all of them, May and Tom quarrelling about nothing, as though they were already an old married couple.

In the *Western Mail* on Monday morning there was news of a young woman attempting suicide by walking out beyond her depth in Tenby. She had been saved by a fisherman who had happened to notice her, dragged her out of the water and taken her to hospital. Lowri and Josi hired a car and visited her that very afternoon.

It was Sali, very wan and ill, still in danger but refusing to answer any questions about Mari Elen. She didn't know what had happened, she didn't know, she didn't care, she wanted to die, she wanted them to go. She turned away from them and eventually the nurse on duty asked them to leave since they were obviously distressing her.

They couldn't leave Tenby. They felt nearer Mari Elen there, even though they had no idea where she was. They contacted the police who promised to let them know if they heard anything, but they still couldn't bring themselves to leave the town. Hoping Tom and May would understand, they decided to stay on in one of the hotels on the front.

After the evening meal they tried to talk to some of the staff. Where would a four-year-old child left on her own in the town be likely to find shelter? Could anyone help them? Did they know of any person who knew just about everything that went on in the town. Some sort of unofficial newsgatherer. Yes, there was such a man and his name was Dai Kyffin. How could they find him? He was usually drinking in one or other of the town's pubs. Everyone knew him. Only get on the right side of him by buying him a drink or two and he would help them for sure. Yes, Dai Kyffin was the man to help them.

They left at once, promising to reward anyone who had helped find the child.

But Dai Kyffin didn't seem to be out that night. They visited one pub after another but no one seemed ready to point him out. At the end of the evening it was the man himself who gave himself up. 'Heard about how you wanted my help,' he said, his eyes watering and seeming short sighted. 'Aye, Dai's your man,' he said. 'A pint or two and I'm at your service, Sir and Madam. A pint or two will set me up nice.'

They bought him a pint and promised the second as soon as he'd given them some news. Lowri was looking in his direction as though he was really going to be their saviour and even Josi felt more optimistic that he had during the whole long day.

'Now then,' Dai said, 'A little miss around four years old. All right, any more information? How was she dressed? Was she looking very smart? Could a person have sold her dress for a tidy little sum of money, now? You see, I do know a lady in the second-hand clothing trade. I could go and see whether she'd spotted this smart little four year old. She'd be very kind to her, I can assure you of that. She's not got a nasty bone in her body. Nell's the name, she's in the second-hand clothing business. If she haven't seen the little miss, she'll know who has. Nell have got second sight. And what she'd appreciate, Sir, is a half-pint bottle of stout. She'd really perk up if a body was to take her a half-pint bottle of stout. Oh, thank you, kind Sir. And another pint of the best for me, Sir, and then I'll be on my way. I'll report back to you, Sir, in half an hour. Thank you Sir and Madam both.'

'He knows all that goes on around here,' the landlord told them. 'Whoever put you up to look out for old Dai knew his business. Now then, what for the lady? A drink of port will be better for her than lemonade, Sir. I can see that the lady is having a stressful time and lemonade, Sir, doesn't do anything for stress. Right, port and lemon for the lady and another pint for the gentleman. You wait here for Dai. Dai Kyffin won't let you down.'

After the second port and lemon, Lowri became very emotional and tearful and Josi decided to take her back to the hotel. He'd wait for Dai and wait all night if necessary.

What a night it was. Josi felt that he'd like to break every bone in Sali's body. She was looking so small and helpless in the hospital, but she had tried to ruin their life with her wild accusations. She had apologised to May for hurting her, but nothing would make her retract her statement that she was Mari Elen's mother. Did she really believe such rubbish? Was she quite mad? He thought of her again, that pale reddish hair, that sweet face so like Lowri's and that implacable spirit. He'd like – well, to be able to save her, he supposed, to restore her to sanity. Who could do that? It needed a better man than him. Graham was interested in the mind, but Graham was too impatient and angry. He could do her no good.

It was almost closing time before Dai turned up. No, he had no definite news but he promised to have a word here and a word there and if she was in the town he'd let them know by ten o'clock the next day. Ten o'clock on the dot. He'd have some news for them. He'd require some money for what he had spent, but nothing more. He was prepared to do everything he could for the lovely lady who was so distressed.

'Good night to you, Sir, and my kindest regards to your lady wife, Sir. Dai Kyffin at your service, Sir.'

The first piece of news came from the hospital. Little Sali had died in the night. 'No, she didn't want to be saved,' the nurse told them, 'no, she was quite determined to die.' She had told the night nurse that she was sorry for all she'd done. Please to tell her sister that she was truly sorry. She had tried to persuade Mari Elen to go into the sea with her but she had refused and gone off in the direction of the town. She hoped Mari Elen was all right.'

Josi held Lowri and they cried together. Josi could hardly believe that Sali had done such a terrible thing. Lowri kept saying that her mother knew how strange and troubled Sali was but had been able to do nothing for her. Their father was dead.

When it was time for Dai Kyffin to appear, they couldn't believe that there could be any good news but there was.

'Oh yes,' he said, 'Nell and me, we've managed to trace the little girl, but we'll have to go very easy now. She's with a woman called Floss, who loves little children, but is liable to be hasty, and you wouldn't want her hasty, you wouldn't want to send the police in for instance because she don't like the police and there's no knowing what she might do. She had a lady's little peke, she did, but when they sent for the police she'd killed the little dog, yes she had, Ma-am, not wanting anyone to get her if she couldn't. Now, what we advise is this. Nell would take your lady wife, all quiet and nice like, to call on the lady called Floss. She's very tender hearted and if she saw how the lady and the child was crying, wantin' to be together, probably she'd be willing to let her go, Ma-am, for a small renumeration for the food, the chips more than anything, because she lives on chips, Ma-am, not able to cook much for herself. Would you be willing, Ma-am? You'd be in no danger I assure you, Nell being a very kind sort of creature and anxious, most anxious I'm sure to reunite mother and child.'

Lowri assured him that she would be very pleased to go with Nell, and indeed Nell was waiting outside to do her bit.

'Well, you see,' Nell said, 'we knows one another from childhood, Floss and me, and I've got my ways and Floss has her ways, but is real tender hearted if approached without force or threats of any kind. I suppose she knows as she should have gone to the police about the little girl, but then Floss don't like the police from way back, so what is one to do. Yes, I knew about the child because she turns to me and asks me about cough medicine and so on, so I know there's someone what she's looking after because she's not coughing much herself and she'd soon get over it if she was. I suggest that you buy Floss a very handsome cake, Ma-am, to get her on your side, she's very partial to fruit cake or cake of any kind and that would be a good way to show her that you've come friendly like.'

Lowri went to the nearest shop and bought a very opulent-looking cake, covered with jam and dessicated coconut, and they went on their way, Lowri fearful and extremely uneasy. Floss' home was down a dark alley, the sort of place Lowri wouldn't have thought existed in such a prosperous town; a large front door with peeling paint and a window with a heavy lace curtain. They stood waiting for her to come to the door. She came.

The hall was full of prams of all sorts, most of them standing on their front wheels to save space. 'I has second-hand clothes as you know and Floss is one of my agents, she stores some of my stuff for me, my house being very small and sheds expensive to come by and mostly damp.'

There was no sign nor sound of Mari Elen. Nell introduced the two women and Lowri thrust the cake into her hands. It seemed like a ridiculously obvious tactic, but it worked.

'Come for the little girl, haven't you?' she asked. 'Well she's been treated very kind as she'll tell you. Only she's not at all well today. She had a very heavy cold when she came after me, Ma-am, when I was getting my supper from Daly's. She said she was hungry and didn't she eat. Without a word of a lie, I had to make do with a piece of bread and scrape that night. But she must have caught cold in the sea. Yes, her little friend had had her in the sea and without no towel to dry herself. She's slept with me in my bed, she hasn't had no cold in my house, but she's not at all well today, I must warn you Ma-am.' She took them through to a room which served as bedroom, sitting room and kitchen and there in the small bed was Mari Elen, half dead and hardly conscious. 'I must get a car to take her away and what do I owe you Madam for all your kindness and care of my little daughter?'

'Ma-am, I won't take a penny, though she has been a little troublesome, but not her fault. Oh, thank you. How very kind. This will really put me back on my feet what with the rent due next week. And you won't go to the police, will you? They'd enjoy having something to charge me with. Don't mention it Ma-am, she's a lovely child who I treated like one of my own.'

Nell had managed to get a taxi and Lowri wrapped the sick child in her own coat and took her out. Nell stayed with Floss but telling Lowri how well she'd behaved. 'You're a real lady, Ma-am and God bless you.' Perhaps she meant to have a share of the gold sovereign Lowri had pressed into her friend's hand.

They arrived back at the hotel to find that Josi had rewarded Dai Kyffin, who at last had been prevailed upon to leave. 'I've felt like someone in a Dickens' novel all day,' Josi said. 'Would you believe that there are still those little mean streets and alleys and those tiny dark houses?'

Lowri couldn't respond. 'She's very hot, Josi. Do you think we can ask Graham to come to fetch us from the station?'

'Of course we can. If I send him a postcard now he'll get it by the afternoon post.'

They bought a postcard of Tenby. 'All's well,' they wrote. 'Mari Elen has a heavy cold or perhaps worse. Can you fetch us from the station please? The three-fifteen train. Yrs Josi and Lowri.'

Mari Elen was very unwell, feverishly speaking of going into the sea and Sali trying to pull her into the water. It really seemed that poor, sick Sali had tried to drown both of them.

'Thank God this one is a little fighter,' Josi said. 'Oh, Lowri what can I do to show you how much I love you? You've suffered as much as I have. You're a wonderful woman. I married you thinking you were a sweet young girl, but I find that I've married a marvellous woman, wise and courageous. Mari Elen will be proud of you.'

Something of Josi's anguish woke Mari Elen. She started to cry piteously. 'Sali was my real mother and now she's dead.'

The little girl was suddenly shaking with an attack of violent grief, crying and wailing.

'You're absolutely wrong, cariad. Your real mother was a lovely woman called Miriam Lewis who died. It's been wrong of me to try to hide that from you. As soon as you're better I'll tell you all about her. She was a teacher in Rhydfelen school and all the children loved her. She was very clever and sang beautifully. Lowri married me so that she could love you and look after you. You love her too, don't you?'

'Oh yes, I do. I'm glad Sali was not my real mother because she tried to drown me. Lowri would never do that, would you Lowri?'

'Sali was very sick, cariad,' Lowri said. 'She was so sick she didn't know what she was saying or what she was doing. We all have to try to forgive her.'

'I've got a very bad throat and my head is throbbing. I want a drink, but I can't swallow. The lady called Floss put cold water in a flannel on my forehead and that was very nice. She was very kind to me and cried so much when I was ill.'

'We gave her money for looking after you and you shall send her a nice present when you're better. Graham is coming to fetch us from the train and because he's a doctor he will know what to do to make you better.'

'She promised she'd let me take the cat out in one of her prams when I was better. I'd have liked that.'

Lowri bought a woollen blanket to wrap her in and Josi carried her to the station for the midday train. He kept it from Lowri but he was terrified by the heat coming from the child's body. She slept almost all the way back.

'Do you think it could be diptheria?'

'Let's not speculate until Graham sees her. It may be only a very heavy cold.'

They both knew that it was something far more serious than a mere cold.

Graham met them, he didn't seem as worried as they'd expected and when he said she had pneumonia they were comforted. Pneumonia was something they had known and dealt with, they knew people, Nano and Tom, for instance, who had pulled through attacks of pneumonia, whereas diptheria and scarlet fever were something alien and more frightening.

All the same the little girl was very ill. It seemed to comfort Lowri's mother to help nurse her; her little Sali had gone, but helping to keep Mari Elen alive seemed to ease her pain. She was willing and eager to sit with the patient at any time during the night so that Lowri and Josi could have some sleep. For over a week Mari Elen was in danger, but on the following Sunday night she sat up in bed and called out for bread and butter and a cup of milk. And demanded to know why everyone was crying. She seemed to have forgotten her ordeal. Sali wasn't mentioned, neither was Floss, neither was the sea; she was back with them as though she had never been away.

Sali's funeral took place very quietly. The fisherman who had tried to save her life came to her funeral. He seemed to be utterly distraught that the young girl he had managed to save had later died. He became very friendly with Lowri's mother, he was a bachelor whose mother had recently died and in no time at all she had agreed to go to Tenby to be his housekeeper. At first Lowri wasn't happy about the arrangement; she wanted to put Tenby out of her mind for ever. But gradually she got to like Arthur Williams and felt that something good had come out of the whole sorry episode. He called to see Mari Elen and painted a picture for her, a black and white cow at a gate. He was a competent artist and when it was too rough to go to sea he painted postcards which he sold to the tourists. Mari Elen loved her cow whom she called Betsan and would often ask after the big bearded man who had painted it. Later, it seemed to be the only thing she remembered of her long illness.

When she came downstairs for the first time, she had lost all her baby fat and was two or three inches taller, her hair, becoming tangled because of her fever, had been cut short and curled around her head. 'My goodness,' Tom said, 'she was a pretty little girl, yes, but now she's a beauty.'

'She looks like Miriam,' Lowri said softly.

'She was my mother, wasn't she?' Mari Elen asked. She must have been thinking of the girl who had pretended to be her mother, but she didn't mention her. How much was locked into her little head, Josi wondered.

Yes, she was going to be a real beauty. Catrin's face was too perfect, she lacked that one salient point that made people stare, but Mari Elen had her mother's smile and her downward glance, she was going to make men suffer, no doubt about that.

Josi looked at her and shivered. How she would put them through it, and he too old to fight. The affairs of the last few days had made him look old. Tom saw that he wasn't such a large man as he'd always appeared to be; he was hardly taller than Tom himself, but something about his father's great spirit, his ebulliance, had lent him inches. Suddenly it occurred to him that Lowri had married an old man. Well, if she had, she certainly seemed to dote on him, so that was all right.

'May and I want you and Catrin to be matrons of honour at our wedding,' he told Lowri. 'We must put this episode behind us and look forward now. We're going to be married in London in the New Year and we want all the family with us. Mari Elen shall be the bridesmaid with you two keeping her in order. And baby Rachel shall wear her grandmother's christening gown and her great-grandmother's shawl and she won't cry all day.' Baby Rachel turned to Tom and smiled at him. It was her first real smile, it was a miracle. It was taken as a smile for a wedding.

'I'm glad I don't have to wear a very, very old white dress,' Mari Elen said. 'I'm going to Regent Street to get my outfit. That's very near Buckingham Palace where the king lives,' she told them.

'I'm frightened of this one already,' Josi said. 'And I

haven't got five hundred pounds to play with.'

'Ah, but the bride's father pays for the bridesmaids' dresses. One day up in Town and my doting father will pick up the bill for the four of us, that's the bride's father's prerogative. And he'll pay for a wedding breakfast in the Ritz as well. Oh, we'll have a wonderful day. Tom talks about having a secret wedding, just the two of us and the family. Well, I'd love that. But I'm all my poor old father's got and he'll want it to be an occasion to remember. All his relatives will be there and his neighbours will be invited in to see the photographs. It will keep him happy for years.'

'Or at least until the birth of the son and heir,' Catrin said.

Chapter eleven

After a few days spent getting over all the trauma and sadness of the previous week, there was more excitement. Tom got an official letter telling him that he was going to be awarded a Military Cross for extreme bravery. 'For outstanding gallantry in bringing in the wounded under fire.' For the duration of the morning, Tom was pleased, indeed almost proud of the honour, but as the day wore on he became more and more truculent and angry.

'How dare they say I was brave? I did nothing except get myself wounded. I did nothing except what I had to do. There were dozens of soldiers who were far more valiant than I was, some of them were recklessly unconcerned about their own welfare; I was extremely cautious on every occasion. I was always as slow to obey an order as I could possibly be, I never once rushed even to help others. I always put myself first and indeed scorned those who seemed to have no thoughts for their own survival. There were heroes, yes, plenty of them, but I was never one of them. I shall refuse the medal of course and all the nonsense which would come with it. Yes, Catrin, I'm quite determined on that.'

Josi was the only person who could understand his point of view.

'I agree with you, lad, that it would be playing false to accept some honour that you didn't deserve. All the same I think you should think a bit longer about your lack of merit. Perhaps your cool apparent lack of concern was what kept the others from panicking. I'm not saying you should accept it, I'm only advocating that you should think about it a little longer.'

Catrin and Lowri were also disappointed that Tom felt he needed to refuse the honour. They both felt they'd enjoy boasting about his bravery.

Not a word was said during lunch, Mari Elen wasn't even told about the affair though she seemed to suspect that there was something wrong. 'Have you had a quarrel?' she asked them all. 'If so, please make it up, I feel uncomfortable.'

'We haven't had a quarrel,' May said, 'But we all think Tom is being a bit stupid.'

'You think I'm being stupid?' he asked her in a hurt voice.

'Very. You see, I want you to take it. I want to be married to Lt Tom Evans MC. These medals may be petty and silly but who are you to decide what you deserved or didn't deserve? If a mistake has been made, and I very much doubt it, then it's somebody else's error. You didn't ask for it. I want you to take it.'

'The lady has spoken,' Tom said. 'How can I deny her

anything? Of course I'll write saying I feel honoured etc.'

'Fancy that, Mari Elen,' Lowri said 'Your brother will have a medal from the king in Buckingham Palace.'

'I want to come too,' Mari Elen said. 'I've never been to Buckingham Palace.'

'It won't entail a trip to Buckingham Palace or anything like that. But if it does, you shall certainly come with us,' May said.

There was no further discussion. Catrin and Lowri looked at one another with little tight smiles. She's clipped your wings, my lad, Josi thought, but said nothing.

May was charming but she had a firm mind which reminded him of Rachel's. If Rachel decided on anything, neither he nor anyone else could get her to change her mind. She's clipped your wings, lad, he thought again.

'There's definitely no date in Buckingham Palace anyway,' Tom said as an afterthought. 'If I were still on active service, I'd have a little ribbon on my tunic. That's all. The actual cross will probably come much later, possibly after the war.'

'If you come to London with me,' May said to Mari Elen, 'so that I can buy my dress and yours, I'll take you to look at Buckingham Palace afterwards. How's that?'

'Oh, thank you. Will I stay a night with you?'

'I hope so, two or three would be better.'

'I'm not sure about staying a night unless Lowri comes too. I sometimes have nasty dreams.'

They all looked at her anxiously. She never mentioned her dreadful experiences, but she must still be suffering.

'If Lowri came too, it would be absolutely perfect. And I'd only ask you to stay one night because I know how busy she is.'

'And I'm busy, too. I have lots and lots of jobs to do, don't I, Lowri?'

'You certainly do. But I think Maud and Lottie will manage for one day.'

May's father was even more delighted about the military honour than his daughter. He sent Tom a letter.

To have a son-in-law wounded in the service of his country is thrilling but the fact that he's also the recipient of a Military Cross makes me the happiest man alive. May has mentioned your determination to master driving a car and it will obviously be a particular godsend for you. Will you do me the honour of accepting a motor car from me as a token of my pride. I have a Daimler – not the same model as the king – and they assure me that they can adapt the same one for you because I have found it most reliable. May will drop me a line to tell me that you agree. Please agree, dear Tom. If you do, I'll save you the trouble of coming up to London to ask for my daughter's hand. Precious as she is to me, I'm now certain that you have deserved her. How's that for magnanimity? With best wishes to you and all your family.

Lawrence Malcolm.

'How generous,' Tom said. 'It would surely be churlish not to accept. And I must say that at the present time I'd find it difficult to justify buying any car let alone a Daimler which, even I know, is particularly splendid. I must write to thank your father this afternoon.'

Lowri and Mari Elen had their day's shopping in the West End and brought home beautiful dresses, Mari Elen's was very pale pink and flouncy with tiny rosebuds in darker pink on the sash and Lowri's was apple-green silk and very plain.

'There were much prettier dresses for Lowri in the shop. Some had frills and lace. I don't know why she didn't listen to me.'

'What did you choose for her?' Josi asked. 'I wish I could have been with you. I bet I'd have been on your side.'

'The one I liked best was dark blue watered silk with lace on the bodice and four wide frills all the way down from the bodice to the hem. It was really beautiful.'

'It was beautiful,' Lowri said, ' but I don't think it suited me. You see, I certainly could never have worn it on any other occasion. But I'll be able to wear the pale green to all sorts of functions: weddings, christenings, parties; and it fitted perfectly without any alteration.'

The Prossers' new house was being built, Gwenllian was particularly thrilled to be having a bedroom of her own.

'And what do we do with Brithdir?' Josi asked. 'Pull it down and sell the bricks, they're home-made bricks, I know we could get something for them.'

Maudie was laying supper in the dining room. 'Oh, Mr Ifans,' she said, 'excuse me listening to your conversation. Please don't pull Brithdir down. John Charles and I want to get married and he works for a builder and he could try to put it right in his spare time. We'd love to live in Brithdir, or even in a part of it, and I'd still be able to come over here every day.'

'But you're very young to be getting married, Maudie,' Tom said.

'I know I am, Mr Tom, only just eighteen, but I'm getting older all the time and John Charles…'

She failed to finish her sentence. She was a big, golden-haired girl in her prime and Tom was young enough to know what John Charles had in mind.

'I'm not pretending it was all him either,' she told Tom later when they were alone together. 'I mean I wasn't forced, don't think that. I mean I'd accepted the feel of his body, the shape of it, I mean, and by the time I wanted to stop he wouldn't stop and he said that was my fault, too.'

'It wasn't your fault,' Tom said, 'that's all I want to say. There's nothing else to say, nothing else to concern me.'

'Thank you,' Maudie said in a choked voice. She seemed aware that she'd already said too much.

'And, well,' Tom continued, 'if John Charles undertakes to see to the roof and the general repairs then you can certainly rent it. Perhaps we can look forward to a spring wedding?'

'I'm afraid we need to get married before the spring, Mr Tom. If you understand me.'

'Of course. Well, the sooner the better then, I suppose.'

'Thank you, Mr Tom. Oh, thank you. I'll be able to tell my parents now. Thank you.'

Later that evening, Tom told his father about Maud.

'Well, it's the way of the world, Tom,' Josi said. ' It's how it's always been, I suppose. As long as the man shoulders his responsibilities, I can't think why the chapel insists on regarding it as such a sin. I'm afraid I sinned a fair amount in my early life, what about you?'

'No', Tom said. 'There's been very little sinning in mine. In France you could go and pay for it if you chose to. But I never did. To tell you the truth I'm fairly lacking in the sinning department.'

Josi went on looking at him. He seemed to have more he wanted to say.

'I've sinned in my head of course,' Tom added. 'And that's as bad, according to the Bible.'

'Women are so beautiful,' Josi said, 'and one or two have beauty of soul as well.'

'I wasn't looking for anything like that. I wasn't looking for anything really. But I remember, even when I was twelve or so, waiting by those rails where you can see the back stairs to watch the maids going up to bed. That's all. Looking and just imagining them getting undressed.' Tom sighed. 'Do you remember that girl called Ceridwen something? Ceridwen Morris. She was not exactly fat, but full in that very sensuous way and in the lamplight her black hair had red flames in it. I was in the kitchen once – she knew I was there – and there was just a drop of sherry left in one of the decanters and she tipped it back into her mouth and I watched it slurping down her white throat and after she had swallowed it she looked over at me and laughed. She seemed to be challenging me in some way, perhaps only daring me to tell mother, but it seemed more, much more than that. I couldn't sleep that night. Fourteen, fifteen, how old was I? I don't remember. I was innocent except in my mind. And I suppose I'm not so different now.' He sighed again.

Chapter twelve

When Tom was called in to see his bank manager, he thought he was in for an easy ride. He wasn't aware of spending any large sums of money, the five hundred sovereigns was paying in full for the building work and the remainder would be very useful to pay his share of the wedding ceremony. He went in with his head held high.

The first thing dealt with was his medal, his bravery. 'Well done lad. The whole locality is proud of you and I feel honoured to be dealing with your financial affairs.' A long awkward pause. 'However they are in rather a perilous state at the moment and I must warn you that you'll have to make some really large changes as soon as possible.'

'Great Heavens, what's all this about? I didn't think we were living differently from how we've always lived.'

'Perhaps not, but now your capital has been eaten away and you can no longer afford to run the farm without it making a healthy profit.'

'Doesn't the farm at least pay for itself?'

'It hasn't for many years. Where do you imagine your

profit comes from? Your living costs far outweigh what you make by your cattle sales and very little goes to market.'

'We've always bred pedigree cattle. Some of our young bulls go to Ireland and England, they're really sought after. My father and Mr Prosser can give you the exact figures, but I'm always astonished by the deals they make. And our heifers always do remarkably well.'

'I have the figures. The sales are a drop in the ocean. You've even put up your wages. No other farmer in the district has been so generous.'

'They're all paid far too little. We had a good harvest this year.'

'Most of your crops are kept for feed, though, isn't that so? You sell skimmed milk to the biscuit factory in Rhosymaen instead of selling a regular supply of milk to the dairies.'

'We send eggs to the mart every week.'

'That's pin money. You've got to change your lifestyle, Mr Evans, I'm afraid. You've always lived like gentry, but you can't go on in that way without coming to grief. I can't even advise you to sell some land, because you'd have to be doing it every year. You see how it's been with me: always aware of your situation. Your charming mother dying and that was no time to bring all this on to your poor father. Then, when I was about to raise the matter again, you were off to war. Your farming is nothing but an expensive hobby, Mr Evans. I suggest you sell up and take up golf instead.

'What can I do?' Tom could scarcely speak.

'Wasn't there talk of you becoming a solicitor?'

'No, I didn't finish my time at Oxford. I wasn't a scholar. I certainly didn't like law. All I ever wanted was the farm.'

'You could do a year's training and become a teacher, I suppose. Oh, but the farm would be too expensive a hobby for a teacher.'

'And I'm getting married in February. And I can't see what changes we can make.'

'Cefn Hebog is just about paying its way now that your father has let it, but Hendre Ddu is losing more and more every month.'

'And you see how helpless I am. Can't pull my weight, nothing but a liability.'

The man took over from the bank manager. 'All is not lost. If you talk it over sensibly with your family some savings can certainly be made, but what is really needed is some change of direction, some scheme that will put you on your feet again. You could become an auctioneer, perhaps. Your knowledge of livestock is considerable and it seems very easy to hold one's own when it comes to things like household furniture and effects. Of course you'd have to buy your way in and pay off that considerable loan, so you'd struggle for several years. But there's a good living to be made and, if I may say so, you've got the necessary looks and voice for the job. People like someone with the gift of the gab and who's a bit of a toff as well. Go to the mart on Wednesday morning and watch old Humphrey Watkins at it. People go there for the entertainment.'

'We'll think of something. I'll keep in touch.'

'And congratulations on your forthcoming wedding, my boy. Sorry to have cast a blight on the proceedings.'

They were a very sombre gathering at supper that night.

'Bank managers are noted for their damned pessimism,' Josi said. 'It's probably not nearly as bad as he's made out. All right, it means tightening our belts in whatever ways we can. Proceed with caution. Right?'

Lowri spoke up, 'And however can we send full cream milk to the market? We use twelve pounds of butter every week and everybody knows that you can't make butter without cream.'

'I agree with you,' Tom said. 'And I'd like to see Tada's face if we were sent in damson tart one day without a jug of cream.'

'Eating well is one of the principles of a good life, it keeps a man healthy and happy and sane,' Josi said.

'We've just got to think of other ways,' Lowri said. 'Now Lottie makes wonderful Welsh cakes in no time at all. Maudie and I are pretty good with sultana scones and cheese scones. We could try to find out what profit we'd make if Maud and Lottie went to the market on Thursday morning. Half a dozen fruit cakes as well. Is that a good idea?'

'Tom could start painting again. His mother thought he was a wonderful artist.'

'Every mother thinks her son is wonderful in every way,' Tom said crossly. 'It doesn't mean a thing.'

'You had the Arnold Webster cup in your school, I remember that. And I know I've been amazed at the prices of little watercolours in that Hammond Art Shop in Castle Street. Five pounds for tiny things no bigger than the ones you used to paint for your mother every Christmas.'

They all turned and scrutinised the little watercolours over the sideboard; one of hills with a red brick cottage in the distance, one of a bridge over a stream.

'I bet you could paint one of those every day. It would do you good, plenty of fresh air. I often think the old barn needs to be recorded before it falls down. It's sixteenth century so that architect fellow told us. You and Catrin were always painting and drawing when you were children. You were both supposed to have great talent.'

'There was nothing else to do here when it was too wet to go out. And Mother kept us well supplied with paints and paper. She'd been fond of painting when she was young and in that school in Malvern that Tadcu sent her to.'

'I bet you could make quite a lot of money if you worked hard.'

'Nobody would pay for such amateur work. You've certainly made me want to have a try again, but I'm sure there'd be no real money in it. Edward and I used to belong to a sketching club at Oxford. We all used to cycle out and find picturesque scenes. He and I thought we were pretty good, I must say, but we were probably no better than all the rest.'

'Just try it. Catrin's left masses of good paper and watercolours and brushes up in the attic,' Lowri said. 'I think it does sound a good idea. I'd hate to think of you having to be an auctioneer and having to make silly jokes about women's hats and so on. I don't think you'd be any good at it, either. Your father would be a natural; flirting with the women and the young girls, but not you.'

Josi looked ruefully at his wife. 'You're becoming altogether too cheeky young Lowri,' he told her tenderly. 'Anyway, a man doesn't flirt when he has all he wants at home.'

Tom was pleased to note the warmth between them.

'I'll give it a go,' he said, 'though I don't think I'll make any more money than Lottie and Maudie going to the market. I'll go to speak to that Archie Hammond, anyway. Take him one or two of my latest paintings. I doubt he'll seriously consider them. And what would he give me for them? He'd want his percentage you can be sure of that. If I work hard I may get two or three pounds a week, I suppose. How much does a teacher earn?'

No one seemed to know much about earning money. Two or three pounds a week seemed a fortune to Lowri; when she was a maid she'd had fifteen pounds a year. Surely you could feed a family on two or three pounds a week? But it was those overheads that worried her, what were they exactly? Anyway, she felt glad that May had gone back to London. There was no need for her to know about their money worries. Though perhaps she would have money of her own.

'I wonder if May has money,' she asked innocently. She'd thought of it so she might as well ask, that's how Lowri was.

'I've no idea. But we could hardly live on May's money, could we?'

'Oh no. I was only thinking of hats and stockings and so on, her personal things.'

Josi pulled her to him and bit her ear lobe. 'How much do you spend every year on stockings and hats and so on?' he asked her.

'I had new shoes last year and they were five and sixpence.'

'Great Heavens, no wonder our finances are in this state. These women will be the ruin of us. Thank goodness Catrin has found a rich fellow. Doctors are always rich. Do you think he'd lend us money if it were a real emergency?'

'I hope it doesn't come to that,' Tom said. 'Let's go to bed. Finances were never my strong point. I'm ashamed to admit that I've still got some debts to certain wine merchants in Oxford. All the same, I'm pretty sure they're all much richer than I am.'

'Even I can see the flaw in that statement, but on your conscience be it,' Josi replied, but without undue concern.

The next morning Tom got the framed pictures down from the wall of the dining room as well as the two larger ones from the sitting room.

'Isn't that one Catrin's?' Lowri asked him.

'Is it? Never mind, it looks like mine, green upon green, and I'm sure Catrin won't mind. Now I have to wrap them all in newspaper and…'

'Only dust them properly first,' Lowri said. 'Look, I'll get a damp cloth and get the smears off the glass.'

'I think perhaps the smears improve them. I don't want anyone to study them too closely.'

'They're wonderful,' Lowri said with passion in her voice. 'Especially Catrin's,' she added when she got to the door.

Graham called for Tom on Friday morning, promising to wait for him outside the shop until he'd finished negotiations.

Naturally Mr Hammond was not as enthusiastic as the family, but he did say he would accept three of the eight paintings Tom showed him. 'I'll send the larger one to our Chelsea showroom,' he said. 'I'm only now a very small part of the Loseley and Hammond team, we have branches in Henley-on-Arden and Stow in the Cotswolds. I'll let them set the price; it will be far more than I would dare ask here and you, of course, will receive seventy-five per cent of the amount realised.'

'And have you any idea what that might be?'

'I wouldn't be surprised if they might ask ten or twelve guineas. Of course I shall only ask three or four guineas for these two. I think you have more talent than most water colourists, but unfortunately my clients won't recognise that. Yes, by all means show me more. I'll accept one or two and perhaps even send another to London if it's as good as this one. There is also a dealer I could recommend in the Hayes in Cardiff, a Lewis Arthur Morgan. He and I have a good working relationship. I try to interest him in my new clients and I'll mention you to him.'

'Thank you. My brother-in-law, Dr Andrews, is waiting for me now, so I'd better make a move. I expect to have a motor car of my own quite soon, which will make me independent.'

'Excellent. I wish you well.'

'He seemed a decent sort of bloke,' Tom told Graham as he joined him in the car.

'Why didn't he take all the paintings then? He doesn't seem very enthusiastic.'

'He's sending one to their gallery in Chelsea and he thinks it may get ten or twelve guineas.'

'Very good. Straight home now, or have we got time for a drink in The Bell?'

'By all means. A celebration drink, yes by all means.' Suddenly Tom felt that he knew what he wanted to do with the rest of his life. He didn't want to be a teacher or an auctioneer, he wanted to be an artist. He felt like an artist. He felt he wanted to paint every hill and tree they passed.

'I'm going to be an artist,' he told his father when he got home.

'Good. But being an artist is no good in itself. Being a succesful, famous, rich artist is the challenge.'

'I'll be all of those things, you shall see.'

He felt so sorry that he hadn't gone to an art school instead of to a university. If he'd have suggested it, his mother might have given way, she thought both her children showed great talent in drawing and painting. Instead of that, he had done exactly what his headmaster had suggested without thinking where it might lead. He had certainly never wanted to be a lawyer. It was Catrin who had set her heart on art school and might have got there if it hadn't been for the war which had made her turn to nursing instead. He was ashamed of how strongly he had opposed Catrin's wish to go to the Slade, having read about art students who cut their hair to look like men, and believed in free love. Poor Catrin, he had got his wish. She had married and settled down but might she still be hankering after a different sort of life, one full of romance and danger? He hoped with all his heart that she was feeling at least fairly happy, fairly resigned to the routine of her life in the country.

His work had changed. The colours were deeper, they were no longer as innocent. From the new paintings, one had the feeling that the countryside held menace, shadows were dark, skies were threatening. Lowri wasn't entirely happy at the result of the first morning's work. 'They're not pictures I'd want to live with, somehow. They make me think of bad days and uneasy dreams.' Josi felt the same. 'Listen, lad, you've got to sell these pictures. You've got to listen to your public, that's Lowri and me. We think you've lost something. Perhaps you're trying too hard.'

But Mr Hammond was delighted with what he'd done. 'You've reached a new dimension,' is what he said. 'You've looked at the countryside, my boy, here or in France. These are mature works. There's a brooding quality about them which the critics will seize upon. These paintings of hills, meadows, rivers, dark clouds, convey a deep melancholy and unrest which suggest 1917. With these and more like them I think you'll make your mark. On, on, my boy.'

'Yes, Mr Hammond liked them,' was all he told Lowri and Josi that night, but he was filled with hope and determination. He now felt he had something to live for.

The following week, May still in London buying her trousseau and visiting relatives to invite them to her February wedding, something very strange happened to Tom. It was a cold, bright day and he was well wrapped up, but instead of taking out his pad and his watercolours, he pulled out some large sheets of paper and some charcoal and started to draw scenes he remembered from the trenches. His concentration was so deep that he missed the bell rung for dinner and Josi came out to see if something had happened to him. He could hardly bear to leave his drawings, couldn't say much to anyone during the meal, was only anxious to get back.

'He's drawing some of the war scenes that are still in his mind,' Josi told Lowri.

'And in my nightmares,' Tom added.

'Well done, lad. Whether they sell or not, I feel you're doing something really worthwhile.'

'Dreadful things they are,' Josi told Lowri after Tom had gone back to work. 'Dreadful, dark things, all black with some patches of dark red; blood I suppose and some red petals strewn here and there. But mostly bodies, living and dead, some of them a horrible greenish colour. A corpse being sucked into the mud. Terrible things. Nothing anyone would like to look at, let alone pay good money for.'

At the end of the week, Tom was rather concerned at the prospect of showing Mr Hammond what he'd been doing, but he needn't have worried. Mr Hammond was so impressed that he said he was going to ask Mr Loseley, the head of the firm, to come down to have a look at his work.

'He's already promised to visit to look at one or two other things I'm interested in. Try to produce one or two of these again next week so that I'll have half a dozen to show him if he comes the following weekend. If he's as impressed by these as I am, he might accept some for an exhibition of war paintings he's arranging for the spring. That would really get you started. Thomas Lloyd Evans. I think you told me that Lloyd is your second name. I think Tom Evans sounds too abrupt. And names are important. Tom Lloyd Evans? T Lloyd Evans? What do you think?'

'I've written Tom Evans on this batch. That's my signature. I think it sounds good.'

'Very well. My latest protégé, Tom Evans. My latest find, Tom Evans.'

'I think I found you as a matter of fact, but we won't quarrel about that.'

'Lieutenant Tom Evans MC. Yes, you see I've been researching your background. Llandovery College and Jesus College, Oxford, I believe.'

'That's right. Came down without a degree though and I'm convinced my MC was awarded simply because I lost my leg and not for any particular gallantry. I think it's best that we stick to art, don't you?'

'Not at all, young man. You paint and I'll do the marketing. Is that a deal? I've been in this business for forty years, my lad. Trust me. Half the paintings we sell will be for that MC. People will want an authentic part of the action. Trust me, young man.'

'I'm also the proud owner of a new Daimler motor car. Is that of importance?'

'No. But I'm delighted that you're now independent. Good luck with your driving. Do you like Goya's work, Tom? Is he an influence?'

'Don't know his work I'm afraid.'

'I think you do. And I feel he's been a big influence on your development. Trust me. Look, take this book with you and you'll see what I mean.'

'I've entered the world of marketing, cheating and lies,' Tom told Josi and Lowri over dinner that day. 'Hammond is writing me up as someone greatly influenced by an artist I've never come across.'

'Did he like the dark drawings then?' Lowri asked.

'Yes he certainly did. Wants another couple before next weekend. Talks of exhibiting some in a big London gallery along with some other war artists.'

'My word. Will you be famous, then?'

'Yes. Mari Elen will be proud of me yet.'

'I am proud of you. I had to go out to the front of the class to tell everybody that you had won a medal in the war and Miss Bacon said I must be very proud.'

'Is Miss Bacon a nice teacher?'

'Yes she is. She's quite pretty too, but the boys call her Miss Pig. That's not kind is it?'

'Very unkind. I hope you don't.' Tom said.

'No I don't. Though she is sometimes cross with me.'

'Do you talk too much?'

'Yes, and I sometimes pinch Ceri because she's prettier than me.'

'Mari Elen, no one could be prettier than you.'

'She is, she's got blue eyes and yellow hair and little fat arms. She looks like a doll.'

'I could never give my heart to a girl with little fat arms.'

'You've given your heart to May. I hope she has pretty arms.'

'She has. I made sure of that. Do you realise that it's only two months to my wedding. Are you looking forward to it?'

'Yes, only I have Christmas to think of first. It's a very busy time, Lowri says, and I must help a lot. Luckily, we have a holiday from school, so I shall be helping Lottie and Maud all day long. Sorry, but I have to go back to school now. I'll talk some more when I get back.'

I'm sure you will, Tom thought. Whatever is going to become of this child? She's sharp as a blade and she seems more like ten years old than three.

After dinner, when Lowri walked her back to school, Tom asked Josi whether he and Catrin had been as clever as Mari Elen.

'Great Heavens no. Mari Elen is frighteningly bright, isn't she. She reads words in English and Welsh already and she reckons things out like a preacher. Talking of preachers, she has man-to-man discussions with Mr Isaacs. "It's not that I don't believe you," she says, "but I can't work it out, somehow." She's just too much for Lowri and me. We're simple folk and all we want is a quiet life.'

Chapter thirteen

Tom found it impossible to stop working. Graham, as his doctor, feared he was doing far too much.

'You'll use up all your memories and dreams in a couple of weeks if you're not careful. Get it all out of your system, by all means, but you must consider your health which is the most important thing. No one should work as you're doing. Mornings only would be my rule, nine until twelve. May won't want to marry an invalid. Now that you've got a motor car you should get about a bit. Get to know the coastline in Cardiganshire and Pembrokeshire. When this war phase passes you may want to paint seascapes; they're always popular with the tourists. What about a painting of the little cathedral in St David's? What about the ruins at Ystrad Fflur? The sailors' church at Mwnt? Get out, find the scenes you'll want to paint in the spring. I don't want to have to treat you for a nervous breakdown. Go easy on the war memories. They must be fading now.'

Tom looked at him as though he were mad. 'Yes,' he said, 'I suppose they might fade. In time. Anyway, Graham, thank you for your advice which I'll endeavour to follow. After this week it'll be mornings only, I promise you.'

May and her father were coming to spend Christmas with Tom and his family so of course the meals and all the arrangements had to be perfect. The new housekeeper, Lowri's aunt, worked like a slave, but poor Maud was sick and could hardly help at all. On Christmas Eve, after they had arrived on the afternoon train, the festivities began. Since Mr Malcolm and May were members of the church, it was decided that they should all go to midnight mass, even Mari Elen being allowed to accompany them. She fell asleep during the short service and Mr Malcolm was the one she chose to be allowed to carry her home. After that he was her devoted servant and the two became very close for the rest of his stay.

'Did I tell you about the time my real mother died?' she asked him on Christmas afternoon. 'Well, it was a very stormy night and by a dreadful mistake she was locked out of the house and had to stay in the churchyard all night. When day dawned she found the church door had been left open so she went in to the church which was decorated with white and green flowers exactly as it was last night. And in the morning the vicar found her amongst all the flowers. She was so beautiful that he couldn't believe that she was dead. He raised her in his arms and kissed her closed eyelids but she was never to wake again. Then he went to tell my father what had happened to his wife. "You shouldn't have locked her out of the house," he said. "You have verily caused her death." My father was bowed down with grief. But he soon recovered and afterwards married Lowri to be my step-mother. I love Lowri very much but she is not as beautiful as my real mother, who was called Miriam.'

'That's a beautiful story,' Mr Malcolm said, 'but I think, madam, that you were making it up as you went along. Perhaps you will be a famous author when you grow up.'

'I can't decide whether to be a famous author or a famous artist like my half-brother, Tom. People are very enthusiastic about his work though I think it is rather ugly. I shall only paint beautiful things about death and churches and lilies.'

'Anyone think it was a mistake to have taken her to midnight mass last night?' Josi asked. 'If you remember I was in favour of leaving her at home with Maud. How long will this churches and lilies phase last? I could do without it.'

Mari Elen seemed to have fallen in love with Mr Malcolm. It was laughable how she insisted on sitting next to him and lavishing her attention on him. Josi felt sorry for the man and wondered whether he'd ever before had such devotion shown him. 'Will you come for a walk with me? Would you like to be my Grandpa because I haven't got a Grandpa? Shall I sit next to you at the wedding party? Shall I sit next to you at the carol service tonight? Would you like to nurse my new baby? She's really only a doll but I like to pretend that she's a real baby. Look, she cries when I turn her upside down or pat her on the back. Was May a nice little girl when she was only three and a half like me? Was she prettier than me? Did you like her more than you like me?'

'Let poor Mr Malcolm have five minutes to himself, Mari Elen. He doesn't have to play with you all day.'

'Oh, but he's leaving on Wednesday and I shall miss him so much. Mr Malcolm, do you promise to come again at Easter? I wish you lived with us and could be my Tadcu, that's Welsh for Grandpa. That would make me so happy.' She patted his face and held his hand in hers.

'Don't be silly, he's delighted at all the attention,' May said when Lowri tried to apologise for the way Mari Elen was behaving. 'He's absolutely besotted with the child,' she assured them, but Lowri and Josi found it hard to believe. Lawrence Malcolm was a thin, ailing man with no obvious attractions, but for Mari Elen he was a knight, a very perfect gentleman. She never let him out of her sight.

He and May had bought her an impressive post office set for Christmas but when Mr Malcolm had found that he was elevated to Grandpa status he insisted on taking Mari Elen to the best shop in Carmarthen and buying her a long white party dress with pearl headdress and a black velvet cape. It had an enormous effect on Mari Elen, turning her into a perfect little lady. She wore nothing else for the whole of the Christmas holiday.

When Tom next visited Mr Hammond with two new drawings, the dealer had some excellent news. Mr Loseley had been as impressed by his work as he himself was and intended showing some of his paintings in the gallery's new-year exhibition of contemporary artists. 'He puts you second to none,' Mr Hammond said. 'One of the real discoveries of 1918. He will be inviting all the critics in before the exhibition opens and of course they will all be told about your war service and your Military Cross.'

May was very excited and invited them all to come up to London to visit the exhibition on the opening night, staying with her and her father afterwards. Josi said that only Mari Elen could go as she was the only one with suitable clothes. 'We'll all have suitable clothes,' Lowri said. 'You've got to get a new suit for the wedding so you can wear it once beforehand. I'm certainly going. By the way, Catrin wondered if you could invite Rose to the wedding. They've written to each other once or twice and get on so well.'

'Of course she must come. I shall look forward to meeting her and so will my father. Are you sure there's no one else from Wales who you would like to invite? It'll be nothing but all my relatives, I'm afraid, all my maiden aunts and my great-aunts.'

There were eight of Tom's drawings in the exhibition as well as two of his earlier paintings. When Josi and Lowri, having put Mari Elen to bed, joined Tom and May at the gallery they found that each one of his drawings had a red circle at its side. 'Every one has been sold,' May said excitedly. 'It may be partly due to the article in *The Times* this morning that said that Siegfried Sassoon's great war poems had been illustrated at last and by another MC, Tom Evans, exciting new artist from Wales.'

'Would you believe one hundred guineas?' Tom whispered to his father.

'Surely not,' Josi said. 'The world is going mad. To

think... well, I won't tell you what I thought about that particular one.'

Rose was at the exhibition and she and Catrin got very emotional together. 'Did you recognise the dead soldier?' Rose asked Catrin. 'It wasn't anyone from his own company, it was Edward each time.'

'Yes, that was the first thing I noticed. In each of the drawings. He must have missed him as much as we did.'

'Have you heard of this poet whose poems are supposed to have the same impact as Tom's drawings?'

'Yes. He got into trouble some time ago, calling for an immediate end to hostilities. He would probably have been jailed, disgraced certainly, except that his friends declared he was suffering a nervous breakdown, over-tired, over-emotional, overwhelmed I suppose, and therefore not able to think straight. He was pardoned, I believe and they say he's insisting on going out to France again. But whatever his opinions are, his poems still stand. They're wonderful. And I think Tom has been invited to meet him before he goes back to the Front.'

'Do you think Tom is aware of how everyone is talking about him? How handsome he is. He's taller and he's filled out since the last time I saw him. How wonderful that he's alive. So many of Edward's friends have been killed. I must find Tom to tell him how pleased I am to see him again and to find him alive.'

Mr Hammond rounded up all Tom's friends and gave them all a glass of champagne. Catrin and Rose both cried a little, but it was hardly noticed. Rose had to leave, she had re-married and her husband was waiting for her, but not before she'd promised to visit them in the spring.

'She and I loved the same man,' Catrin told May. 'I'll tell you about it one day. He was Tom's friend and he's the soldier who lies dead or mutilated in some of the drawings. He was so handsome. May, you wouldn't have noticed Tom if Edward was around.'

The poet, Sassoon, who'd been classed with Tom in *The Times* review turned up and congratulated Tom on his drawings. 'It's like being back in those bloody trenches. You're lucky to be out of it. I return next month. Tell me, is the dying soldier you show in so many of your drawings a man called Edward Turncliffe?'

'Yes. We were never together in the same battles, never even in the same regiment. He died in one of the first battles in Ypres, but he was a very good friend and I think of him far too often.'

'I didn't know him at all well but we were neighbours and I always admired his looks, so to see him tonight has been a real surprise. I mustn't take up too much of your time, but I hope we meet again.'

Before leaving, Tom found that Siegfried Sassoon had bought one of his drawings. He felt very proud of that.

They returned to Hendre Ddu early next morning and soon Tom forgot that he was an exhibited artist. The money, though, was a godsend.

'You know, Lowri' Josi said when they were in bed that night, 'I can't help feeling a bit worried about Catrin. I mean, all this great fuss about Tom. After all, it was her that was supposed to be the artist, wasn't it?'

There was a moment's silence.

'Yes, you're right.' Another pause. 'But don't worry yourself about it. Her talent is safe inside her and she'll use it again one day.'

'I hope so,' Josi said, rather doubtfully. 'I'll have to tell her something like that anyway. Yes.'

Lowri hadn't finished. 'I don't think Jesus Christ thought too much about having babies and so on in that parable about the talents. About people using their talents and not burying them.'

Josi was taken aback. Lowri had obviously imbibed more than good housekeeping from Nano. Though Nano, of course, would only have praised the Good Lord, would never, Heaven forbid, have doubted Him. He felt the need to steer the subject in a safer direction. 'I never quite understood that parable,' he said at last, trying to keep his voice steady. 'And I had a very good Sunday School teacher too. Old Ifor Davies, the farrier. I suppose you're too young to remember Ifor Davies? Father of Arnold and Dai?

But there was no answer. Lowri was asleep.

One morning Maudie turned up for work a sorry sight. Her pretty face was swollen and she had two black eyes. 'What happened?' Tom asked her. 'Now please don't tell me that you bumped into a door. I am your friend, I want to look after you, I want you to tell me the truth.'

'John Charles has a terrible temper and last night I wouldn't do what he asked me.' She burst into tears.

'Do you mind, Maud, if I go to speak to your father?'

'No, Mr Tom. I'd appreciate it. He and my mother are very worried about me.'

Tom drove the short distance to their small cottage, he was too impatient to walk.

'She mustn't get married Mr Williams. She mustn't get married to a bully. If he's like this even before they're wed, what will he be like afterwards?'

'But he wants to do the right thing, he offered to marry her, we didn't have to put any pressure on him.'

'I don't like the lad and I don't think you should accept his offer. We'd be very pleased if she remained with us, we can give her her own room so that she can keep the child as well.'

'Would you really do that for her, Mister Tom?'

'We'd be glad to. She's a good girl. And she shouldn't have to suffer for one mistake. We all know how our feelings can get the better of us sometimes and how persuasive a young man can be. She's too good a girl to marry an oaf. If he decides to change, to make himself worthy of her, then we might consider his offer at some future time. But I'd prefer it if she found someone else, some decent lad.'

'We could have her back here with us, Mister Tom.'

'No, I think you're a bit crowded here as it is. I'm not so sure that you wouldn't do better to live in Prosser's old house if I got it mended for you. It's got three bedrooms, though two are quite small.'

'That would be wonderful. Old Jack Garnant our landlord won't do a thing and won't buy us any materials so that we could try to make some repairs ourselves.'

'Right. You can come and see it tomorrow but you'll have to wait for at least a couple of weeks before it will be ready for you. I've got a couple of men working on it.'

'And can I lend a hand, like? I've done a fair bit of bricklaying and some carpentry. Can I see what I can do in the evenings?'

'Splendid. Come to look over the place tomorrow and if you like it, two of my men will bring the horse and cart to help you with the move.'

'Right,' Tom told Maudie when he arrived back. 'You are staying on here. Lottie shall have her own little room so that you can have the baby in with you and your parents are coming to live in Prosser's old house so that you'll have plenty of helpers with the baby. How's that?'

Maudie couldn't answer, but the look she gave Tom seemed thanks enough.

'I'm only worried that you seem to be rewarding immoral behaviour,' Mr Isaacs the minister told Tom on Sunday morning. 'I know the chapel has been too hard in the past, but all the same there is a happy mean.'

'I understand what you're saying, Mr Isaacs,' Tom said, 'but Maudie is a good girl who got into the clutches of a bully. They were immoral and I don't condone that, but you see they were about to wed, and anyway I won't have her beaten up by anyone. I don't think she'll make the same mistake again. You may come to talk to her tomorrow afternoon if you'd like to. When you see her poor face you won't think we've been too lenient. She's a good girl, Mr Isaacs, and a very good worker.'

Josi thought that Tom would have finished with war drawings but he hadn't. He was still hard at it most days as though they were something he needed to work through. An occasional one would be much less harsh, would show men at work burying the dead, with pity and grief clearly shown in their faces. It was as though he were trying to say that the horrors of war, the frequency of death, are never acceptable, but that, all the same, it brings out a great deal of pity and tenderness in the soldiers.

One of his drawings showed the prelude to the football match which had taken place in the first Christmas of the war. Tom had not been present of course, and what he tried to show was not the actual game but the preparation for it, the rather uneasy faces of the Germans and the English who had respect and pity for one another. He wondered whether a poem had been written about that event. For him it showed the worst aspect of war, how men were having to kill other men whom they felt friendly towards and pitied.

During his short talk with Sassoon, the poet, looking rather embarrassed, had pressed into his hands a book of his poetry, *Counter-Attack*; it had a vivid scarlet and mustard-yellow dust jacket, and Tom already had many of the poems by heart. He had never before appreciated poetry, even considered it effeminate, but these pieces were rough and raw, spectacular as the dust jacket.

He stirred shifting his body; then the pain
Leapt like a prowling beast, and gripped and tore
His groping dreams with grinding claws and fangs

They did, in fact, express what his pictures were trying to express; the horror of war. It was a counter-attack to the idea of war as heroic and noble.

At this time Tom felt he was two people; the Tom who was real seemed to be the one who took decisions about the farm and looked forward to his marriage in the near future, but there was another Tom who was an artist, who read and appreciated poetry and even tried to write it. He didn't really believe in this second Tom, it seemed like someone he'd dreamed up and not his real self at all. And yet he went on with his drawings, finding different scenes, some from memory some from dreams, and accepted that they were good.

The wedding day dawned clear and cold. The family went to London on the early train, Catrin, Lowri and Mari Elen taking their dresses with them to change into at May's house. They were all very excited. Tom could hardly believe that only seventy or eighty miles away in France the war was still raging, the battles as unrelenting and bloody as ever. He remembered the time when people had honestly thought it would be all over on that first Christmas but five Christmases had already passed and very little seemed resolved.

The wedding breakfast was quite meagre, the first time that the Hendre Ddu folk had come across the scarcities and hardships that city people were used to. May's relatives seemed bemused by the step May was taking in leaving her father to live in the wilds of Wales, they seemed bemused by Josi who was trying to put them at their ease but not succeeding, as a wedding party they seemed altogether too sedate and quiet. Even the church service had seemed very short and quiet, the joyful wedding hymns sung without joy.

Tom and May were spending a week in Dorset and May's father and the half-a-dozen guests from Wales went to the station at Paddington to see them off. There were many haunted-looking soldiers at the station, either coming home or returning from the Front. 'O my brave, brown companions,' Tom thought, Sassoon's words never far from his mind.

In April Maudie's little son was born, a handsome boy, seven pounds in weight with a fine mop of black hair. She called him Ianto after her favourite sheepdog and he became a firm favourite, spending much of his time with May and Tom.

May hoped that she would also become pregnant, but as the months went by she started to fear that she might be barren. 'Just don't think about it,' Catrin said. 'Graham says he's known of several couples who fail to conceive at first, but when they give it up and stop trying, the woman finds herself pregnant almost immediately.'

It wasn't easy not to think about it. As summer came with still no sign of a baby, May became more and more attached to little Ianto so that Maudie became worried. I know she wants to adopt the boy, Maudie told herself, but I won't let her do that, he's mine.

Maudie's mother begged her to consider the lad's future.

'If they can't have a baby but adopt Ianto, he'd become the heir of Hendre Ddu. What could you hope to give him? I'm not saying it would be easy, but I think it's what you ought to do,' she said.

By this time, there was another young man, Harry Hughes, a teacher in the boys' school in town who'd become interested in Maudie. He knew about Ianto but her mother thought he'd be more likely to propose to her if there was no child. Harry lived with his mother, a very respectable retired teacher, and Maudie's mother felt that she also would be less likely to object to the marriage if there was no child.

'You should think of your chances, Maudie. You may never get another young man interested in you.'

'Nonsense,' her father said. 'She's the prettiest and most hard-working woman in the neighbourhood. Men will always beat a path to her door. I hear what you say about being the heir of Hendre Ddu, but in my opinion a child should stay with its mother. Would you give any of our children up for adoption? There you are then, no more talk about such a thing. Ianto is ours and we're proud of him.'

Tom could do no wrong in the art world. He'd now begun to paint portraits, one of May sitting in the window of the drawing room, one of Catrin with her little daughter, one of Maudie when she was heavily pregnant, her body overflowing but her face still slim and fine. He named it 'Juno' and when it was sold it made more money that any other painting. He was pleased that it had been sold to the museum in Cardiff so that it would be seen and admired by many people for many years.

One day he asked Maudie whether she would like to come with him and May to see the picture in Cardiff. Ianto was left with his grandmother and they set off in the car shortly after breakfast.

Tom was very moved to see his painting in such a prominent position in the museum but Maudie seemed rather embarrassed, the more so because she'd overheard a man telling another, 'That must be his wife, I suppose. It certainly looks as though he cherishes her and quite right too.' She hoped May hadn't heard him.

They had lunch out in a smart restaurant and afterwards Tom bought them a blouse each in Howells Store. It was the first time Maudie had been to a large town or seen such splendid shops. 'And London is even bigger than Cardiff?' She could hardly believe it.

Mari Elen was annoyed that she hadn't been invited to Cardiff. 'If I let you paint a picture of me, will you take me with you to see it?'

'I will, certainly, but you're never willing to sit still for more than about three minutes. If I paint you, you'd have to sit for hours over several days.'

'Then perhaps I'll wait until I'm older.'

Mari Elen was dismayed that Lowri wouldn't let her wear her long bridesmaid dress to the Easter concert at school. It seemed that everyone else was going to be smarter than she was.

'You'll have occasion to wear it again very soon,' Josi said. 'Lowri's mother has let us know that she's getting married if you please, in just three weeks' time. Yes, she's decided that being Arthur Williams' housekeeper is not enough. She says he's a few years younger than she is, but that he's a good chapel-going man and she wants to be his wife.'

'She's almost sixty years old,' Lowri said, 'but never mind, I thought Arthur was a lovely man; he was so upset over poor Sali's death.'

The wedding was to be very quiet with only Lowri, Josi and Mari Elen invited.

Mari Elen looked lovely on the wedding day. They went to Tenby by train and then, because it was raining, Josi ordered a taxi to take them to the chapel. At one point in the journey they were in full view of the sea and it had a traumatic effect on Mari Elen. She became rigid with fear and screamed as though she were being tortured. 'I don't want to go in Tenby,' she cried. 'I want to go home. I'm not going anywhere but home.'

By the time they'd got to the chapel she was white and trembling and refused to go in. For a long time they sat in the car, waiting for her to calm down, but she remained in a sorry state. They could hear the minister beginning the wedding service. 'You go in,' Josi told Lowri at last. 'I'll bring her in as soon as I can. It's not right to force her against her will.'

Lowri hurried into the chapel and Josi paid the taxi. Then, taking Mari Elen in his arms, he turned towards the sea. He felt that his small daughter should meet her demons. In a way he thought it was a good thing that her fears had surfaced. The child had been dragged into the water by a person who swore she was her mother. No wonder she was in a panic. 'What did poor Sali say to you?' he asked very quietly and calmly. 'You know she lied about being your mother. What else did she say?'

It was a long time before Mari Elen could stop crying, the jerk and tear of her great sobs shaking her little body. Josi's shirt front was wet with tears and mucus. He suddenly said, 'What about having one of those big ice creams in a café?'

No, not even a treat of that magnitude could comfort the little girl. When she finally stopped crying, only the occasional huge sob shaking her chest, she said, 'Tell me about my mother. Did you love her? When did she die? I didn't want Sali to be my mother because she wanted us both to drown. That's why I turned away from her and ran out of the sea. The sea was horrible, so rough and cold. I wanted her to come with me but she wouldn't. I called and called "Sali, Sali". But if I couldn't be her little girl, she would drown herself that's what she kept saying.'

'She was a very sick person, she thought she was telling the truth, but it was all in her sick imagination. Nobody took her seriously enough. Nobody realised how dangerous she could be. And you, little love, had to suffer. But Mari Elen, it might do you a lot of good that you've let us know how much you went through. You should never bury things deep down inside you because they make trouble for you later. Now you've told us about what a frightening time you had, you may be able to begin to forget it. What a pity that it's too cold to paddle, then you could begin to enjoy yourself and think of the sea as your friend. Your mother loved the sea. We went to live in a really awful little cottage but she was happy there because she could see the sea outside the front window. I loved her very, very much. One day I'll tell you all about her. Her name was Miriam, but I can't talk of her too much because it wouldn't be fair to Lowri who is such a lovely little wife to me now. You understand that don't you?'

'Yes, I think so. It's like Tom doesn't want May to know that he was once in love with Sali.'

'But he wasn't ever in love with Sali, cariad. That again was her sick mind making up its own sad stories. He was kind to Sali because she was very young and a bit frightened when she started work at Hendre Ddu and she imagined that that kindness was love.'

'I think I would like that ice cream now, Dada.'

'But I think we ought to go back to the chapel now, my love. The wedding service will be over and there'll be a lovely meal prepared for us and you'll want to show your grandmother your new dress. Oh, what a pity, you've made the bodice quite wet. Never mind, if we walk back in this wind it will soon dry. And before we leave Tenby you shall have that ice cream, I promise.'

They were just in time to join the few guests and walk back to Arthur's cottage which was small but very pretty, with white stones decorating the pathway to the front door. Mari Elen fell in love with a tortoiseshell cat nursing two pretty little ginger kittens. 'Please can I have one? Oh, please. My little kitten left Cefn Hebog and went to live in Arwel with the carrier, so please can I have one of these?'

'I think you can,' Lowri's mother said. 'They must be about six weeks old now. Their eyes are turning green and when that happens you know they're ready to leave their mother. Have a ham sandwich, cariad. You're looking so pale. Try to eat something.'

Mari Elen couldn't eat anything. She just looked about her and before long was sitting on Arthur's knee. 'I suppose I must be your Grandad now since I'm married to your step-Grandma. What sort of things does a Grandad get to do? Would you like a little trip out in the bay, just you and me?'

Josi watched her face. At first it expressed panic but then she put her hand into Arthur's and said, 'Yes I would please.'

She didn't have her ice cream after all, but she cuddled her little kitten all the way home and seemed a very happy child, her suffering forgotten.

Chapter fourteen

Tom had a letter from the Front. It was from one of the men in his company, a man from South Wales who obviously found writing difficult and wasn't prepared to waste words.

> *Hope you're better now. Sorry you caught it. You said you were for Labour, Sir. My Dad is standing for Labour and would be glad of your help, you being a toff like. He has a very serious opponent who's for communism, but I remember you saying you wouldn't go that far, because human beings weren't good enough for all-out communism or all-out Christianity. I thought you had it right, too, and I told my Dad about you. Here is his address. Please write to him and please go to support him since you stand for the same thing and I bet you thought the Russians had gone too far as well, all that bloodshed on top of all this.*
>
> *Yours ever, Billy Jones.*

He showed May the letter. 'It makes me wish I'd kept my mouth shut,' he said. 'No it doesn't. I will go to support him. After all, it's what I believe in. My father can remain a Liberal like all his family before him. Oh yes, this is a Liberal stronghold, this is, all the people around here still have pictures of Ewart Gladstone and John Bright on their walls, but I think we must move on and become a great deal more radical, as John Bright was, to give him his due. Seeing the tremendous gap between the officer class and the men made me realise how wrong the whole system is. "The rank is but the guinea's stamp, The man's the gold for a' that." And I want to say so publicly because I may never get another chance. I'll write to Billy's dad and tell him to name the day.'

Tom believed that he would be asked to say a few words of support, to offer a vote of thanks or something of that order. It embarrassed him when he saw a poster in the station. 'Hear Tom Evans MC, famous Welsh artist, talk about his socialist beliefs.' He was to be the main speaker of the evening. For a few minutes he felt sick with apprehension.

He was still very nervous when he got up to address a full and very boisterous audience. 'When I came home from war I started having nightmares. My doctor thought they might become less severe if I spoke about my experiences. But I didn't feel I could. I painted my experiences instead and became an artist. I'm telling you that so that you can understand that I'm no speaker. I wish I could paint what I feel about the best way forward. I believe in a real brotherhood of man, equality, liberty for all from the grinding poverty of the pit; fair wages for the workers. That is no empty slogan but what the Labour Party is all about. Communism sounds wonderfully exciting but I believe it is a dangerous way forward and will lead to anarchy. The slogans are wonderful, I grant you that. "To all according to their needs, from all according to their ability." (There was a great deal of clapping and shouting when he said this.) 'But who will be fair and great enough to see that this is done? It's asking too much of human nature to say that a lazy worker should have exactly the same as the willing industrious worker. It takes away initiative and drive. There can never be absolute equality because some people are more able and more hard-working than others. What Labour supporters insist on is that there should be equality of opportunity, everyone starting from the same place to make what they will of their lives. That's all I have to say. The Sermon on the Mount is too idealistic. Who can live according to Jesus' laws? Chapel-goers? We all know that paying lip-service to an ideal doesn't ensure we live according to those ideals. Communism is another idealistic dogma that won't work because men, as God said after the flood, "are evil in their hearts". During the present war I witnessed acts of great heroism and bravery, men at their best, risking their lives to save a comrade, but the cause of the war was men at their worst, greedy and menacing. That's all I have to say, brothers. As I said, I'm no speaker. I suggest that we now sing "The Red Flag" to be followed by contributions from the floor.'

His speech was greeted by a volley of applause, short speeches were obviously popular. He was popular. They'd heard he was a great artist and they liked great people, especially when they were Welsh and spoke with a Welsh accent not like some men who'd been to Oxford and spoke with clipped English accents that even their parents were ashamed of. There were lively contributions from the floor, especially from the communist contingent, which accused Tom of having no trust in the working man. Eventually the evening was over and Tom was taken to the lodgings that had been found for him with an elderly woman who declared herself a Labour supporter because neither Conservative nor Liberal had remembered to call for her in their official car during the last election. She gave him a tasty supper and then he was glad to go to bed, his first night of campaigning over. The next day when Billy's father called on him to thank him and to escort him to the station, Tom gave him twenty pounds towards the fighting fund. It's only a painting or two, he told himself when he thought May might think him too generous.

'Now you'll come again, won't you,' Billy's father said. 'It would be wonderful to have you here on election night. The sight of you with your missing leg will be a real vote-catcher. You're a handsome man and a bit of a toff and d'you know, the people round here they only pay lip-service to the idea that all men are equal. You'll do us no harm at all.'

Tom managed to escape without making any definite promise. All the same, he hadn't decided against a second visit. All in all, he'd enjoyed the experience and felt surprised that he had managed to talk as well as he had.

He was contacted again, but at the time he was in hospital. He had decided to have a false leg fitted. 'I don't mind not having a leg under my trousers but I hate not having a foot. They'll fit a foot onto my false leg. It probably won't look right, but it will do me good when I get used to it. I know I'll have to practise hard.'

He never understood how the next episode came about. Out of the blue a man called at Hendre Ddu and asked whether he would stand as a Labour candidate in the next local election. 'But everyone stands as independent in the local election,' Josi said, 'it's what you're prepared to do for the electorate which counts, not your political allegiance.'

'Let the boy speak for himself,' the man said. 'No one really knows what Labour means around here. It would be a good way to introduce a new party to a country electorate and it might help when it comes to a parliamentary election.'

'All right, I'll do it,' Tom decided suddenly. 'I don't mind a few meetings in local schools to tell anyone who turns up what I believe in. I won't expect any votes, because people round here are all Liberals to the bone, but I might be able to convince one or two of them that Labour is not a revolutionary party and that they have nothing to fear from us.'

'Oh, it's us now is it?' Josi asked. 'Are you a member of this new party by any chance?'

'Yes I am. May and I joined the party as soon as I came back from Ton-y-Bont. She is as zealous as I am.'

'And why didn't you ask me to join the ranks?'

'Because I knew you were born a Liberal and will die one.'

'Quite right,' Josi said quietly.

'Tell me about the Labour Party,' Maudie said a few evenings later when she was with him and May in the dining room. 'My father said you were going to speak on their behalf and I'd like to help you if I believe in it.'

'I think you would, Maudie. We stand for equality and fair wages for the workers. We are against the class system and believe that any man, rich or poor, is as good as another.'

'So how have the rich become rich, then? Doesn't the fact that some are rich mean that they deserve it? That they've worked extra hard and been extra clever?'

'We don't mind that. What we are against is inherited wealth. That one man is better than another because his family is wealthy and can send him to a private school where the education is better. Equality is what we believe in. We think everyone should have the same chance in life, whatever his father was, the same schools for all, the same medical care for everyone: rich or poor. I don't pretend it will happen overnight, but that is what we believe in.'

'I'm with you then. You can count on me to take round pamphlets and to try to explain to people what you've explained to me. It sounds like good sense.'

'You're my first convert then, Maudie. Thank you.'

'What about me?' May asked. 'I wasn't at all sure until you talked me into it. My father is dead against the Socialists as you know.'

'English people are afraid of anything new; Tory and Whig is all they understand. They think Labour means that everyone with wealth is going to be robbed.'

'I hope they are,' Maudie said. 'Why should some people have everything and others nothing.'

'Now you're speaking like a Red,' Tom said. 'We'd tax the rich but we wouldn't steal their money. Many people are frightened of Labour, thinking they're Bolsheviks, but they're different. When we get into power there won't be revolution.'

'Pity,' Maudie said.

'Maudie, you're too extreme,' May said.

'She's young,' Tom said. 'Let her be.'

'I've tried to tell my father that you have extreme left-wing views,' May told him later, 'but I don't know how he's going to react when he hears that you are actually standing as a Labour candidate.'

'Don't tell him then,' Tom said. 'Look, it's only a local election and I'll get beaten to a pulp, but I'll get some people thinking and that's all I'm hoping for. Don't tell him. It's not important to anyone but us.'

'And will I have to come with you when you make your speeches?'

'I'd like you to, but it might be a bit embarrassing. I daresay I'll have audiences of two or three in some villages.'

Tom was wrong. There was plenty of interest in the meetings, plenty of people wanting to hear about the new party and wanting to see the man who'd become a local hero. They wouldn't go so far as to promise him their vote, but the meetings were all good-natured.

'Now tell us a bit about your part in the war, Mr Ifans,' one of them was sure to say, but he wouldn't be drawn on that subject. All he would say was that the high-ranking officers didn't seem to have much sympathy with the rank and file. All men were equal in his opinion. That's as far as he'd go.

May only went with him once, to the election meeting in the largest village, Brynhir, but Josi would occasionally go with him, 'For the ride, man' he'd say. He would heckle sometimes when he thought things were too quiet, once going as far as to say 'damn-fool nonsense', but Tom knew that Josi's presence would add to his votes; Josi was still an immensely popular figure in the locality.

Occasionally Maudie would propose going with him. She never heckled. On getting to the school, she would clean the blackboard very thoroughly in case he wanted to write on it – he never did – and then watch everyone coming in. When he started to talk she would look at him encouragingly, her mouth slightly open over her slightly protruding front teeth. Tom always enjoyed evenings when she was free to come with him, loved the way she kept her eyes on him, almost without blinking. He suspected that she might be a little in love with him, but he was sure it would do her no harm. It seemed she already had another follower, a very respectable school teacher from Llanfair, so Lottie had told Lowri.

One evening when Josi and he were driving home together, Josi told his son that though, in his opinion, Tom would come last in the election, the Labour party would not let go of him. 'You speak well, even though you're too serious with precious little entertainment value. They'll invite you to take part in the county council election next and I don't think you should.'

'Why not, if I'm doing some good?'

'May doesn't like it, she's afraid of your father-in-law getting to hear of it. Of course I don't care about him, but I do care for May's feelings and I'd hate to see a rift opening between you.'

'Well I suppose you know about rifts between people.'

'Yes, I suppose I deserved that, I did let your mother down in the end, but all the same I gave up a lot when I first got married. And that's the time that two people need each other most.'

Tom realised that his father had something important he wanted to say.

'You don't think May is happy?' he asked.

'I'm not saying that,' was the swift response, 'but I think she could be happier. I've seen her getting to look older in these last weeks and that's always a sign of... well, it's a sign you need to take note of, I suppose. That's all I'm saying, lad. She is after all a devoted wife.'

Tom talked to May about the possibility of his taking part again for the county council and she assured him that she was quite happy about it. Yes, she knew that her father would be hurt, but then again she was fairly sure that he would never get to hear of it.

The war came to an end in November of that year and there were great celebrations everywhere, bonfires lit and a great many speeches about 'the war to end wars'. Tom thought it inconceivable that there should ever be another war; he was convinced that such a thing would be the end of civilisation. 'The numbers of casualties in this war were frightening, any other war would destroy any hope of recovery,' he said.

Mari Elen was dressed up as Britannia in the fancy dress parade and got first prize for the under fives. She got a new half crown in a lovely red satin purse; she pinned it up in her bedroom and swore she would keep it for ever.

At the beginning of the new year, soldiers began to return from the Front, heroes who had no jobs and no hope of any. Nineteen nineteen was a hard year, with flu, as ferocious as the medieval plague, killing millions of people around the world, more even than had been killed in the war.

When they had been married a year, May was more certain than ever that she was barren and started to become really miserable. For her, nothing would ever make up for the fact that she and Tom were childless, she couldn't seem to think of anything else.

'It may be all my fault,' Tom told her. 'How do I know what effect the loss of my leg and all my war experiences have had? I'll go to speak to a specialist about it. Graham will put me in touch with the right man.'

'What I'd like you to do is ask Maudie whether we can adopt Ianto. If she's going to get married in the spring, she'll soon have another child. He's so adorable and he's so happy with us.'

'I didn't know Maudie was getting married in April. Is

she marrying that school teacher after all?'

'I think so. Lottie is full of it. She's going to Carmarthen with her to buy a wedding dress. I'd buy her ten wedding dresses if she agreed to let us adopt little Ianto.'

'You're ready to buy a baby then? Well, I'm not. I'm not convinced we can't have a baby of our own. I'll have to speak to Graham to see what he thinks.'

That night, husband and wife were both very unhappy going to bed. May had really begun to believe that they'd be able to adopt little Ianto and couldn't understand how Tom could oppose her. Tom himself was going through a great crisis. He was racked by his conscience. He'd been unforgiving to his father when, after twenty-three years of marriage, he'd left his mother for Miriam. Now he realised that, after barely a year of marriage, he was sinning in his heart. The idea of lovely Maudie leaving them to get married, even to a decent sort of chap, was more than he could bear. He loved to watch her with her son, loved to watch her washing, baking, carrying trays. He drew little sketches of her and tried to tell himself that all he was was an artist admiring a beautiful woman. He couldn't bear to confess even to himself that he was in love with her, but in his heart he knew he was.

Oh, yes, he loved May too. She was a fine, proud woman, an admirable wife and one day would be an admirable mother. He had to let Maudie leave Hendre Ddu to get married and gradually he had to try to forget her. He certainly wasn't going to agree to the idea of adopting Ianto though, he couldn't deprive the little lad of his rightful mother who was so… who was so beautiful. He bit his arm to try to prevent himself groaning. He'd go out to Arwel woods tomorrow and howl his protests where no one could hear him. He wanted to howl at the thought that she couldn't be his. She couldn't be his. It was the first time he had known what real love was. Not the friendly, brotherly love he felt for May. Why hadn't he realised that what he felt for May was a warm brotherly love, a love as he felt for Catrin? As he had felt for Edward? He had been too inexperienced. He had mistaken mutual loving-kindness for love. Poor Edward had married Rose to save her from a prison sentence when she was a suffragette and he and Catrin had suffered for it. But he himself had had no motive except gratitude that May had written to him faithfully and loyally and had seemed to like him and his family. Nowadays, even making love seemed to have become a duty which was everything to do with a baby's conception and very little to do with urgent physical love. He bit his arm again as he thought… but he wouldn't think. Maud would be leaving Hendre Ddu and he would try his hardest to stop thinking about her. He mustn't think about her, about her sweetness, about her smile which was far too intimate. On the one or two occasions she had come with him when he was addressing a meeting, she'd sat at the front looking at him steadily, so ready to smile when he made some feeble remark. She had the most remarkable eyes, they were pale as water and luminous as sea water with the sun on it. Did she know how he felt? When he offered her his hand to help her get out of the motor car, touching her seemed to set off an electric charge through his body. The touch of her. He couldn't stop thinking about it. About her intelligence, how she would read every book and pamphlet he advised, probably having to read with a candle when she was in bed. He felt giddy at the thought of her lying in bed, her long hazel-coloured hair over her shoulder, her very possibly naked shoulder. He sighed and almost groaned again. He was in a bad way.

And she would marry that school teacher called Harry Hughes who was quite good looking, she said, with chestnut-coloured hair and freckles. And flat feet. It was his flat feet that had kept him from the army. Men with flat feet couldn't march so they had to stay home. Lucky old Harry Hughes, twice lucky old Harry Hughes, to be home and to have his Maudie to love. Stop, stop, oh stop. He was a married man, it was the only the second year of his marriage when love should be powerful and lusty. The word lust made him want to curl up and cry out. May was at his side making small sleep noises from time to time. How could she sleep when he was in torment? Oh, thank God she would never know, never guess what he was going through for Maudie. Even her name was a torment. He felt ashamed of himself, of course he did, and ashamed again for having been so unforgiving towards his father, glad at that time, or at least not exactly sorry, to have had the chance of separating him from his mistress.

The sun was already rising before Tom was able to sleep.

Chapter fifteen

Maudie's mother, Lorna Williams, arrived at the farm early one morning the following week and was shown into the breakfast room. She was a large, handsome woman but she'd obviously been walking too fast so that it was some time before she managed to speak. When she did, it all came out in one breath as though she'd been rehearsing what to say. 'Mister Tom and Mrs Evans, Maudie's great-aunt, that's my husband's auntie, nearly eighty-three she is, has been taken ill with no one to look after her and do the nursing... and Maudie wonders whether she can be spared.'

'Sit down a minute,' Tom said, 'or you'll be needing someone to look after you. Well, of course she can go,' he continued in a moment or two, 'if there's no one else, how can we refuse? But however will she get there? Where does this auntie live? I'm pretty sure it's not around here.'

There was a slight hesitation during which Mrs Williams looked away in some embarrassment. 'Well, Maudie's already gone as a matter of fact, Mister Tom, she knew you wouldn't object. You see, she managed to get a lift from Dai Griff the haulier when she had the afternoon off yesterday. You see, he had a job in the next village and could take her with very little trouble.'

'And have you any idea how long she's likely to be away?'

'Oh, there's no knowing, Mister Tom. As long as it takes, I suppose. She was sure you'd understand.'

'Of course we understand. But what about her marriage plans? Isn't she getting married in a week or two? That's what we've all been told.'

'The wedding is off, Mister Tom.'

'Off? Who called it off? I thought he was a decent sort of chap. He surely hasn't reneged on his promise?'

'He's decent enough and doesn't understand what's happened. None of us do. Who can understand the workings of a young girl's mind? No, it's off and that's all she'll tell us. "Leave the girl alone," my husband says whenever I try to question her. If you ask me she was glad of the excuse to get away to the old lady.'

'And where's Ianto?' May asked, speaking for the first time.

'Oh, he's staying with us. No use taking a baby to a house of sickness.'

'Send him over to keep me company if he's in your way.'

'I will, Mrs Evans. He loves being with you and the boss.'

Tom made an excuse to leave the breakfast table. He felt light headed, so happy he could hardly keep still. He hadn't ridden a horse since returning from France, but he went to the stable and saddled Bessie, a placid old mare he'd scorned to ride when he was fit and young. He sat on her broad back and let her walk on at her own pace. She wasn't getting married, his heart sang out. She's been offered marriage by a decent, sought-after bachelor, but for some reason she'd turned it down. And he knew the reason. He should be ashamed of feeling so happy, but he couldn't help it. She was his and she knew it. They would have to meet and he would have to question her, though he knew her reasons. Her mother had probably guessed the reason too, she had looked strangely at him that morning, often addressing her remarks to May rather than to him.

He was up on the main road and passing the chapel before the truth of the situation broke in on him. She wasn't going to be married to Harry Hughes but that wouldn't make it any easier because he was married and intended to remain as true to his wife as he possibly could. He could look at her, that was all, and she could return the yearning look but that's as far as it could go. She must not give up a decent marriage for so little. Did she realise how little he could give her, he who wanted to give her everything? He had to see her, had to explain to her that though he was in love with her, yes, yes, he was in love with her, he'd admit that much, but in spite of it, they weren't destined to be together but alone and apart for ever. Wouldn't it be better for both of them if she was married and no longer living in Hendre Ddu, no longer seeing each other every day, almost every hour of every day? He had to go to see her. Where did her auntie live? What excuse could he make for going to see her? He could hear his heart thumping in his chest.

He rode slowly along the road past her house. Her mother was out in the orchard by this time, pegging her washing on the line. How could he make conversation? How could he start? 'The rain's keeping off so far,' he said, 'but remember it's still April. There'll be showers before lunch time.'

'Yes indeed the sky's looking quite overcast, but we've got no room to dry anything indoors.'

'Where did you say Maudie's great-aunt lives?'

'In Brynyddol. It's only about twelve miles away but there are no trains in that direction, so she might as well be in London.'

'Well, if you ever need to go to see her you've only got to ask me, and my motor car will be at your service.'

'Well, thank you very much, Mister Tom. I know my husband would be very eager to go to his auntie's funeral if that becomes necessary. She was very good to him when he was a boy and his mother a widow, she pretty well brought him up, I think. Quite a well-known local character she is, Annie Vaughan. Widow to a very respectable seafaring man. Anyone would tell you where she lives.'

Tom felt himself reddening. Maudie's mother seemed to know how things were between him and Maudie without needing to be told. He pulled himself together. There was nothing between himself and Maudie. 'Well, I must be on my way,' he said severely.

Maudie's mother went back to her kitchen, picked up Ianto and hugged him. 'So that's how it is, my darling,' she told him. 'That's why your mother doesn't want to get married. Silly girl. She'll get nothing but misery from Mister Tom because he's a respectable married man. She'll get older and less desirable year by year with nothing to show for it but a silly sly look from time to time and a kiss under the mistletoe at Christmas.'

'Our Maudie's keen on Mister Tom,' she told her husband when he came in for dinner. 'And that's the reason the wedding's off.'

'And who ever gave you that piece of news?'

'Mister Tom was passing by this morning. He told me nothing but he didn't have to. It was written all over his face.'

'Listen to me, girl. Nearly every young married woman has someone she cares for, but he's out of reach so she marries someone else and forgets him.'

'So you're an expert on young married women now are you?'

'No. But I suppose they're very like young married men. There's almost always some impossible dream woman in every young man's life. Marriage and some damn fine times in bed knocks the nonsense out of them. They find that a good down-to-earth partner is what they really wanted all the time.'

'Was that how it was for you?'

'Certainly. I found the right woman and I lived happily with her all my life.'

'Good,' Maudie's mother said, trying not to feel hurt and annoyed.

'Where have you been? I've been looking for you,' May said when Tom returned from the stable.

'I should have told you, love. I suddenly felt like doing a bit of horse riding. Poor old Bessie is as solid as a cart horse but I enjoyed being on her back. I wouldn't dare try a better mount.'

'Did you speak to anyone?'

'Only another word or two with Maudie's mother who was pegging out the washing when I went by.'

'I think Maudie had a real cheek to go to her aunt's without getting our permission first. She's beginning to take advantage of us.'

'But she knew we'd allow her to go. These old people depend on their relatives to look after them when they're sick. They can't afford nurses. Maudie will probably be back quite soon. Apparently the aunt is not expected to live long.'

'As a matter of fact I'm not at all eager for Maudie to come back here. I was glad she was leaving to get married. I think she forgets her place.'

'Do you? I'll have to speak to her about it.'

'I'll have to speak to her about it. She seems to think you're a friend, almost a relative, not her master.'

'I suppose I rather like that. But I'll try to change if it bothers you. I'm sure she doesn't mean to be… overfamiliar.'

'She knows she has a hold over us because we're so keen to adopt Ianto.'

'You're wrong, May. I don't want to adopt Ianto. I wouldn't feel right to deprive her of her son. Perhaps she won't have another. We will have our own child if only you are patient.'

'I don't think so. We've been trying too long by this time. My heart isn't in it any more. In fact I'd like us to have separate rooms, Tom. I've been thinking about it for some time.'

'May, I'm so sorry. Of course I will do what you want, but I must admit that I feel slighted. Think about Lowri. She's younger than you are, love, and they've been married years longer than we have, but she's still optimistic that she will have a baby some day.'

'I think Lowri is mistaken. I'm afraid Josi is too old to father a child now.'

'He fathered Mari Elen not so long ago.'

'Anyway, I don't want to talk about Lowri and Josi. I'm sorry I'm in a bad mood. But I feel slighted by Maudie and I think you're too fond of her. I don't mean that in any wicked way, I simply mean that you allow yourself to be too close to servants who, for that reason, take advantage of us.'

Tom got up hurriedly, left the room without further word and angrily retreated to the small high-ceilinged room which had become his studio. There he immediately picked up his palette and his largest brush and, worked-up as he was, resumed the oil painting he was working on, a painting of Hendre Ddu's old barn. Last week he'd failed to make any headway with it, certain that it wasn't worth trying to rescue, but suddenly he seemed to know exactly what to do. The technique he adopted was something new and adventurous, great angry brush strokes that reminded him of some of the modern art he'd seen in London, but by managing to over-paint the background it seemed to blend in with the rest of the painting. As a result the barn, which was reputed to be far older than any other part of the house, medieval according to some amateur archaeologists who had once called, took on a sinister, mysterious life as though he were suggesting that it was a place where ill deeds, cock-fighting perhaps, or even murder, had taken place. Working feverishly, he finished off the painting in less than an hour. He stood staring at it, stirred by how powerful it seemed, how raw and direct. Could he really be an artist? He often thought that art was a game he was playing simply because he couldn't do much else since his injury, but occasionally he was surprised by something he'd produced which seemed real and true. He stared at this completed work, feeling shaken, almost exalted by it, hardly breathing for several moments.

Once, as a small boy, he'd been very ill with pneumonia, his temperature worryingly high, the doctor calling twice a day. One night, when the fever seemed at its highest, he had stirred and smiled at his mother and Nano at his bedside and from that moment had begun to get better. Telling the story, Nano always insisted that she'd felt a wing beat in the room that night. He and Catrin used to tease her about it. Now he thought about that wing beat.

So impressed he was, so grateful for his undoubted talent, that he was able to return in quite a different mood, humbly apologising to May for storming out. He kissed her fondly and she returned his kiss.

It was about three weeks later that Maudie's mother contacted them to say that her husband's aunt was dead. 'And now I'll have to post Maudie's black suit to her. I told her to take it, but she thought it would be a bad omen.'

'So it would,' Tom said. 'I'll take her clothes over to her if you like. I'm not doing anything important at the moment and it will save you the trouble of making up a parcel and taking it to the Post Office at Llanfair.'

That was the outcome Mrs Williams had been hoping for. 'Would you really Mister Tom? How very kind you are. I'll bring her things over in a bag this afternoon. And could you please find out when she's likely to come home. Oh, and tell her, of course, how the little lad has been asking for her.'

As Tom drove, sedately enough, towards the village where Maudie was staying, he felt that he was flying towards her. All the same he knew he would only be able to stay very briefly, because he was determined to behave in a reserved, sensible way, without referring once to her postponed or cancelled wedding or mention how she was missed at Hendre Ddu. How he missed her.

Maud didn't have the opportunity to rehearse her reaction. When she saw Tom walking up the path to her aunt's cottage she burst into tears, held out her hands to be comforted, put up her face to be kissed. It was completely natural, unpremeditated and moving, childlike rather than flirtatious. Tom said nothing, only he knew he would remember the moment for the rest of his life.

'When is the funeral?' he asked at last in a shaky voice.

'On Friday. Oh, thank you for bringing me my mourning clothes. I was beginning to think I'd have to wear some old black coat belonging to Aunty Annie.'

'And when will you get back? Your mother asked me to find out. She says Ianto has been asking for you.'

'Well, Mister Tom, I'm not quite sure yet whether I will be coming back. Except to pick up all my things. And to get Ianto of course. You see, Aunty Annie has left me this cottage, I didn't even know she owned it. Now before she was ill, she used to keep a little shop in the front parlour and all the neighbours say I should do the same. You see, there isn't another shop in this village and people have to walk two miles to the next village. There's a small school close by for Ianto where he can go when he's three and it's supposed to have a good Mistress too. And all the villagers seem so friendly. They've already been calling here with little parcels of this and that for the funeral tea. Very neighbourly they seem.'

It was all too much for Tom to take in. 'Maudie, I think you're in danger of making a very important decision without enough thought. You really mustn't behave so impulsively at this point. You must come home and talk these things over with your parents. You may not do so well in the shop, not in the first years anyway. It will be such a gamble, you may lose a lot of money. And you have a good place at Hendre Ddu and might well become the housekeeper before too long.'

'But, Tom, I wasn't going to stay at Hendre Ddu in any

case. You know that I was intending to leave at the end of the month.'

Tom forgot his decision not to mention the marriage plans 'Why did you decide not to get married?' he asked. Even that would have meant he would have seen her from time to time, but here she would be really lost to him. 'Why?'

She looked at him miserably. 'You know why,' she said and again burst into tears.

It was the best thing. As he got back into the car he realised how lucky he was. If she was back at the farm and he open to temptation at every turn, how long would his determination to remain faithful to May be likely to last?

Lucky? He found that tears were coursing down his cheeks so that he could hardly drive. When she had cried and held up her face, he had taken advantage of her innocence and kissed her with mounting passion. If she had doubted his feelings for her, she could doubt no more.

He tried to imprint on his memory the way she'd looked that day (when would he see her again?) though she'd looked just as she always looked. As though her clothes were like the clothes on a statue, there only to emphasise the womanly shape of her body, firm breasts, strong sturdy hips. Her blouse was a faded violet-brown, the colour of ploughed fields in February, her long skirt was the grey of water fowls. Browns and greys. He couldn't imagine her in bright colours. Her hair was set in a low circle of plaits at the nape of her neck. Nape was a lovely word. How he'd have loved to lift the heaviness of her hair to kiss the nape of her neck. How he'd love to loosen her hair which was the colour of winter bracken, the burnished autumn colours fading to nutmeg brown. He'd remember her for ever, of course he would.

He had refrained from saying 'I love you', but wasn't it implicit in the way he had kissed her and in the way he had been almost unable to break away from her. He groaned again.

Chapter sixteen

One Saturday morning, a week or two later, Tom came across a very woebegone little figure sitting on the old seat in the orchard. 'Mari Elen, whatever is the matter? Your little face is almost purple. No, stop scrubbing it with your hankie, just look at me and I'll try to help you. Has Tada been cross with you? Or is someone at school being nasty to you?'

It was a long time before she found enough breath to answer. 'Oh no, oh no. It's much worse than that. It's Lowri. It's my little mother. She's… you see she's very ill… she's pregnant.'

'Mari Elen, do you know what being pregnant means?'

'Yes. It means she'll have to go to a sanatorium like poor Edwyn Parry and she'll probably die like he did.'

'Listen to me, you little silly. I promise you that Lowri is not going to die. I'm not going to tell you what being pregnant means, but I'm going to take you indoors, get you to wash your face and then take you to Lowri and she'll explain it to you. All right?'

'All right. Only I heard Tada saying something about her being pregnant and I know she's being sick in the chamber pot because I can hear her, and when I go in her eyes are all blotchy.'

Tom found Lowri upstairs, arranging piles of sheets and pillowcases in the linen cupboard, explained what had happened, then left them together. Afterwards he went outside to find his father.

Josi must have felt that Tom had something on his mind, so he spoke first.

'I had such a shock to see your latest painting in the art shop, lad. You made the old barn look exactly as I've seen it look dozens of times just before a big storm. That's one that should go to London surely.'

'Thanks Nhad. I must say it feels wonderful to know that I really have some talent. At first I thought the art people were being kind because of my war service, but I feel pleasantly self-assured at the moment. At least I have something to feel happy about.'

'You have your mother's gift. I always thought she was a very good amateur artist. That posh school she went to rated her very high.'

Josi's mood suddenly changed, his voice darkening. 'But there are other things you get from me, lad. No doubt about it.'

It was so direct that Tom, who'd have liked to avoid any confrontation, had no choice but to respond. 'You know how it is with me then.'

'I think several people have guessed, but luckily not

May. I don't think she, in her state of purity, could imagine such a thing happening.'

'But I'm not going to do anything about the way I feel. I haven't seen her for a month. She didn't call on us when she came up to fetch Ianto. I still haven't heard from her. It's driving me mad, but I'm afraid if I saw her again I wouldn't be able to resist… wouldn't be able to resist…'

'What a pity you gave in to Nano's last wish. Poor lad, you didn't stand a chance when May came to visit us. She so gracious, so like your dear mother. And you so green, so inexperienced. Anyway, I applaud your determination to make a success of your marriage.' There was a moment's silence. 'Though I can't honestly say that I regret my failure.'

'How could you when Mari Elen is one of the results of it? She's as bright as morning. Only, precocious as she is, she isn't too sure what being pregnant means.'

'Don't speak in riddles, lad. What are you getting at?'

'I believe Lowri is pregnant, Nhad, am I right? If so, my fondest congratulations.'

He explained about his recent encounter with Mari Elen in the orchard. For a moment Josi smiled, then grew serious again.

'We're afraid to say anything, lad, because the poor love has had several miscarriages during these last few years. I insisted that she told Graham last time and he examined her to see if everything was all right, so I suppose Catrin knows about it. I've got a feeling, though, that the first stage this time has lasted a little longer than usual. But I don't intend to make a family announcement until Graham gives us the nod.'

'How wonderful. I do hope she's looking after herself. It will give May a bit of a boost too, I think. She's so anxious to have a baby. And I think having a family of my own might do something for me, too.'

'I hope so. It kept me relatively steady at least until you'd grown up.'

'I never asked you, never had the nerve I suppose, how long you'd been with Miriam before she got pregnant.'

'Why is it suddenly important?'

'I'm interested that's all.'

'Several years all told.'

Tom thought that was all his father was going to say, but after a moment or two he continued. 'I'd heard that the new Mistress of the village school was a fine musician and when Catrin was in the grammar school I went there to ask her whether she'd coach her for the Saint David's Day Eisteddfod at the Grammar School.'

'And that's when it started.'

Josi, tangled in his memories, again failed to answer, looking about him as though trying to remember. 'No. No, not then. She'd have nothing to do with my suggestion. Sent me away feeling very sorry for myself.' Another few moments. 'My, but Nano was furious about it. "Who does she think she is? A chit of a village schoolmistress being so high and mighty."'

That was as much as Josi was ready to disclose. His eyes were suddenly full of tears and Tom left him to himself.

Love rules us all, Tom thought, but I've got to prove I can master it. He went back to May and held some skeins of wool for her to wind into balls. He tried to think of something kind to say but he only managed to tell her how much he liked her new saffron-yellow blouse.

But she had some news for him. 'Catrin called when you were out. You and I are to be uncle and aunt again it seems.'

'How splendid. Little Rachel needs a companion.'

'Yes, she was born on my first visit here. I'm very happy for her and Graham, of course, but very sad about myself.'

'Of course you are. But Graham was telling me that no one should feel over-anxious for at least the first two years. And May, we've barely been married a year and a half.'

'Yes, but I'm a lot older than Catrin, almost ten years older and I don't feel at all optimistic.'

'How about a holiday? Let's go to stay by the sea in Pembrokeshire, somewhere near St David's. We'll spend our days walking along the cliff paths, breathing in the healthy sea air. You'll have to buy a lot of new clothes and we'll pretend we're on our honeymoon.'

'You're very kind to me.'

'Of course I am, I'm your devoted husband.' He kissed her tenderly and felt better than he had for weeks.

After dinner, Tom sought out his father again. 'May tells me that Catrin is expecting another child.'

'Yes, I heard. Poor Graham is very worried apparently, he was frightened to the bone by that depression she had after little Rachel May was born. Catrin could be the same this time again or even worse. He was dead against them having another child. But there you are, even doctors, it seems, can't stop the flow of life.'

'If Lowri is pregnant, and indeed this morning she did have that far-away look in her eyes that I've noticed before in pregnant women, then Catrin could come to live here for a while so that they could be together. To be with Lowri would be the best tonic in the world for Catrin. I'm afraid she isn't altogether happy with Graham. He's a distant sort of fellow isn't he? Very upright and dutiful and wonderfully good, they say, to the poor in the parish. But there's something lacking. An inability to relax and be loving. He never laughs, have you ever noticed that? Hardly ever smiles.'

'We're a strange family, lad. Catrin married Graham because he was so kind and patient to poor Rachel and happened to be around when she had the news of Edward's death. I married Rachel, oh, she was nice looking, almost beautiful at times and rather grand, but it was mostly because I wanted to spite her father who was so much against it. You married May simply because, due to a whim of Nano's, she turned up here, was nice looking and had many good qualities.'

'Why didn't you warn me against it?'

'Would you have thanked me at the time? No, I'm afraid it's what happens, lad. Neither of us had the courage to wait for true love. But I suppose few marriages are really the union of two ecstatic people. Poor little Lowri married me because she was afraid of being parted from Mari Elen.'

'And you were the Mishtir. That probably counted. She'd probably always admired you from afar.'

'But I was also a relative of her mother's, don't forget, so I don't think that sort of admiration went very deep. I was only Josi Ifans, Cefn Hebog to her. And I hadn't got a very good record where marriage was concerned either. Poor little Lowri. I've become very fond of her. Perhaps I'm talking a lot of rubbish, but that's how it is for me. Lowri's a stalwart little creature and she often delights me, I've become very fond of her. But Miriam, well Miriam left a scent on my life and I still long for her at times.'

'And what about poor May? She was sent for, wasn't she, and came to the wilds of Wales simply because she'd had the grace to write weekly letters to me when I was abroad. And suddenly she was promising to marry me.'

'And I think she was pleased to do so. She'd nursed her sick mother for years, had never, according to what she told me, had much chance to make friends and she was thirty, don't forget. It sounds ungracious to say this, but I think she jumped at the chance to be mistress of Hendre Ddu.'

'I wonder what she really thinks of me. All she seems to want is a family. As you say, she never had any friends and she's delighted to have Lowri and Catrin who both seem to have taken to her.'

'My father arranged a marriage at one time.'

Tom loved his father's tales about his father, Jasper Evans, a cheerful, hard-working farmer who seemed to have had a very full and interesting life. 'It was like this; our next-door neighbour, I say next door though her cottage was over half a mile from Cefn Hebog, her name was Gladys Stanley and she had a tidy little cottage and a field with a cow and some chickens. She was in her late thirties by the time I'm talking about and used to come up to call on us from time to time when she'd made herself nervous about some horrific story in the newspaper she took every weekend. My father told her she should get married to have someone to look after her but she always said, "Oh, it's too late now"'.

'Well, one Saturday afternoon he had to call in at Caffreys, the hardware shop in Llanfair, and this very helpful assistant he always went to was dressed in a black suit; his mother had died he said. He told my father he'd lived with her all his life and that he was very lonely. "Get your bike and be ready to come up the hill with me at four o'clock. I'll introduce you to a very nice woman who might interest you." To my father's surprise he accepted the invitation and when they'd pushed their bikes up the hill for three miles, he took the man to Gladys' cottage, knocked on the door and introduced them. "Here's Tom Ifor Lewis," he told her. "He's lonely because his mother's just died. If you give him a nice bowl of cawl and make him a pancake afterwards, he'll probably start calling on you every Saturday night. I'll be glad of his company and I think you will too."

'That's all he had to say. And the two of them must have hit it off very well because a month or so later they called the banns. My father was always very proud of that. They were a very happy couple it seems.'

'It's a good story anyway,' Tom said.

'Absolutely true according to my father. I heard it from him many times.'

Tom looked over at his father and smiled. 'By the way, I'm taking May off for a holiday, suggesting that all the sea air in Pembrokeshire might be the answer to our failure to conceive.'

'Good luck to you. It's a good place to paint too, they say. The air has some special quality, though the air around here seems good enough for me. And it may well be a good place to forget what you need to forget.'

'I'll never forget Maudie, you'll never forget Miriam and I'm afraid Catrin will never forget Edward. But it's better not to drop out of life altogether, isn't it? It's wiser to carry on. I intend to carry on.'

'You're right, son. It's been good to talk things over, but we won't mention any of these things again.'

Within a week or two, Graham had been able to confirm that Lowri was pregnant. Everyone was happy, particularly Catrin. They found out that their babies would be born within a few weeks of each another. Rachel May would be almost two and a half by the time the new baby arrived, Catrin wanted another girl. Mari Elen wanted a girl for them too – or a boy.

Graham agreed that Catrin should spend the last two months of her pregnancy at Hendre Ddu; he too thought it a good idea and of course little Rachel May and Molly the nursemaid would stay as well. Tom was looking forward to it.

He and Catrin had become very close after being so distant as children. Now, their closeness was very important to both of them.

Rachel was a dear little child, plump and very self-contained. She had straight brown hair and big dark eyes, she was pretty enough, but not beautiful like Catrin. She loved to sit on her mother's knee and look calmly around her at everything going on. She adored Mari Elen, but was a little nervous of her, prefering to watch her than to play with her. She was two and a half by this time and would be very good natured and attentive to any younger brother or sister; jealousy was definitely not going to be a problem for Catrin and Graham.

Mari Elen was tremendously excited to hear of her new brother or sister but very unwilling to wait so long for the birth. Josi wondered if he could ever love a new baby as he loved Mari Elen. He was certainly fond of his grand-daughter, complaining bitterly whenever Graham was too busy to bring them over for their Sunday visit. 'You only live five miles away and you could be in Canada for all we get to see you,' he would say.

'Tada we'll be there next Sunday I promise you.'

Rachel was fond of him, too, and called him taxi, the nearest she could get to tadcu. Yes he certainly loved little Rachel, but when he thought of his love for Mari Elen, it seemed to swell in his breast and cause him pain.

It was the beginning of September before Tom and May set out for Pembrokeshire. Tom felt homesick as soon as he'd left his home patch, but reminded himself that it wasn't anything he was doing for himself, but for May. He hadn't even packed any art material apart from a couple of pencils and a packet of plain postcards, the most he was going to do was some sketching.

The boarding house they stayed at was homely and welcoming, the meals excellent. They walked for almost two hours every morning, May always ready to match her pace to his. They found pretty shells and stones on the sandy beaches and occasionally a delightful café where they stopped for morning coffee and bara brith. They got on well, the weather was kind, the sea sparkling outside their window every morning when they woke. Tom persuaded his wife to sketch with him and found that she was talented and would often manage to find some arresting feature in the landscape which he had missed. He realised that though he had been dreading the time they would have to spend together it was passing very pleasantly. Of course there were many times when his thoughts turned to Maudie and at those times he found it difficult not to show his unhappiness. Still, those moods eventually passed and he felt more at ease with himself than he had for a long time. He was delighted that May seemed happy and seemed to welcome their love-making in the little bedroom where they could hear the sea crashing against the rocks and sometimes feel part of it.

They stayed away for three weeks. Tom had been afraid that they'd get bored with each other, they'd never before been so long on their own, but he found May a very interesting person with definite points of view and a clear mind. He hoped that he, too, lived up to her expectations.

Apart from his occasional times of passionate longing for Maudie, which sometimes seemed a real physical pain, he felt that they'd managed to have a happy holiday.

But unfortunately it wasn't a successful one. Before they'd been home a fortnight, May discovered that she was not pregnant, a frightful disappointment especially as her sister-in-law and her step-mother-in-law were beginning to show signs of their pregnancy. And though Catrin and Lowri both tried their best not to show how happy they were, there were times when she could hear them talking and giggling in another room, so that she had to rush upstairs to cry in the privacy of her bedroom.

Josi still went on saying that there was no problem, that he knew many couples who had had no luck for two years, but by this time had a flourishing family and, though May smiled at him once or twice through tears and pretended to believe him, she knew in her heart that she would never conceive. It became the only thing she could think of. Sometimes she felt she was going mad.

Chapter seventeen

One morning in late September Lottie had a strange piece of news for Lowri. 'You know that Harry Hughes, the school teacher who was courting Maudie? Well, honestly, everybody's talking about him. He sold all the good furniture his mother had for him and he's bought a motor car. Honestly. Who ever heard of a school teacher having a motor car? Well, they're only for doctors and lawyers and rich farmers aren't they. Teachers have bicycles, don't they? Everyone is making fun of him and saying it's only that he's trying to impress Maudie Williams. He'll be able to motor down there now and worry the poor girl to death. It's hard enough to say no to a decent man once, isn't it, and now she'll probably have to go through the same thing every Saturday and Sunday. But perhaps she'll say yes, now that he's got a car. It's a small square sort of car, mind, not at all like Mister Tom's.'

'I don't think Maudie will have him,' Lowri said, 'motor car or not. I think she has her mind set on someone else, though I don't know who.'

'Yes,' Lottie agreed. 'But that one was married, I believe, and she's too sensible a girl to waste too much time on someone out of her reach. I wouldn't anyway. I only wish that Harry Hughes would look my way. I'd have him like a shot, though his face is covered with ginger freckles, though quite pale ginger in the winter. But a motor car would make up for those and his red hair.'

Lowri smiled and made an excuse to leave the kitchen.

'Josi,' she whispered to her husband in bed that night. 'Harry Hughes has sold all his mother's good furniture and bought himself a motor car.'

'Well, good for him. Do I know this Harry Hughes, say?'

'Of course you do. He was the school teacher at Llanfair Boys' School who wanted to marry Maudie.'

'Right. And do we have to concern ourselves about him and his motor car?'

'They say he's bought it so that he can continue to chase after poor Maudie.'

'I see. If poor Maudie was still here with us I would certainly try to protect her from any unwanted admirer, but with her over at Brynyddol and it being well gone my usual bedtime, I don't feel I can do much at the moment. Perhaps you'll kindly talk to me about it again when I'm properly awake.'

'Oh, Josi, you are a silly old thing and I do love you. I'm the luckiest woman of all, I'm sure of that.'

Eventually Tom got to hear of Harry Hughes' motor car. 'She can never be mine, so why should I care who's courting her?' he said to himself. But of course his heart felt as though it was being stabbed every time he heard of her. And he hated – and envied – his rival. Sometimes he wished she would marry this school teacher Hughes so that she would come back to live in Llanfair and that he might visit them from time to time. Would that be possible? But he didn't know whether seeing her would ease his pain or increase it. His mind was in turmoil.

At last he wrote her a short, a very short, letter. 'I feel the same as ever. I married too soon but must live with that. Dearest girl, there is no alternative.'

He felt he was giving her her freedom, though it hurt him to do so. He felt tormented and waited for a reply from her. But there wasn't one. He asked Lottie after Harry Hughes from time to time and she thought he was still courting her every weekend.

The only time he felt at peace was when a painting was going particularly well so that he could feel he had something to live for. He never doubted now that he was, or certainly would become, a prominent artist. Another exhibition of his work was planned for London in December and this time it would be showing several paintings as well as the many black and white charcoal studies of trench warfare. He was still suffering from occasional nightmares and getting these scenes down on large sheets of paper was still the best way he knew of dealing with them.

He knew his political life was over. Officials in the Labour Party had let him know that if he stood as parliamentary candidate in Carmarthenshire and did well, though coming last in the polls after the Liberals and Conservatives, he could well be invited to represent Labour in one of the safe Labour seats in the South Wales mining area. May had objected to that, saying it would hurt and offend her father deeply, and Tom had felt secretly relieved. He knew that there were other men from the area who would be better informed than he was and, unlike him, would be prepared to give it all they had. Life as a member of parliament, dividing his time between London and a constituency in South Wales, held no attraction for Tom. He was a countryman, loved his home acres and never wanted to move from them. Even beautiful Pembrokeshire with its sandy coves and gorse-covered cliffs wasn't as dear to him as the fields and cwms of Hendre Ddu. He'd found a way of remaining on his farm and though the money from his painting was not guaranteed, that one traumatic visit to the bank had meant that the farm was gradually becoming more self-sufficient. No other maid had been employed to replace Maudie, Lowri was working hard as always and even May who had never before had to turn her hand to housework was becoming interested in cooking and was encouraged to do her share.

Politics was still of the utmost importance to him and he still gave all the money he could to the Labour Party. He was filled with despair that the soldiers who had served so gallantly and suffered so much hardship were, on being repatriated, finding themselves without jobs and without hope. One of his latest charcoal drawings was of a dole queue; it was inspired by a newspaper photograph, but the men in his picture were the soldiers he remembered from his company, the tough little 'mynufferni' men from South Wales he had admired so much for their political fervour. He called it 1919 and it eventually became the first of his drawings to break the five hundred pound barrier. He gave all the money that picture earned to the Unemployment Fund. As it turned out it was also one of the last of his black and white drawings.

He had become obsessed with colour and with painting in oils. And his paintings were full of the discoveries he was making. One distinguished reviewer said that the influence of the Fauves, the French 'wild beasts', was strong on his work. It was only then that he started finding examples of their work in Cardiff and was proud to be thought to be in that tradition. He spent hours finding out how the proximity of one strong colour changed another and the effect that had on a painting. He would spend a morning dabbling with colour, learning which became lighter and which deeper in conjunction with another and they were wonderful mornings. As a result of all his experiments he learnt to produce some remarkable effects of great boldness and vitality. After returning from holiday he had turned his hand to painting flowers from the garden, the colourful autumn dahlias and canna lilies, and managed to produce a wonderful luminosity so that May said, 'You can smell those flowers and see the dew on them'.

He feared he could never be a great artist because he'd had no training in an art school, had not learnt any theories of technique or colour, had never copied from the old masters, but he was hopeful that he could, at least, become a good artist. He realised that luck had played a big part in his early success, that Hammond had taken him on largely because he was a wounded soldier and an MC. He was convinced that his work had become much better over the last two years, but he wasn't sure that the public would remain loyal and buy the new paintings. Still, he was enjoying all the experimentation and the new work. He found that when he went to Arwel woods and stood sketching and studying its colours he might go home and choose different colours altogether, might add paths where there weren't any because they helped the rhythm of the composition. And he realised as he went on with the painting that he wasn't depicting what he had seen but what he felt about those woods he had known since childhood. And yet he knew better than to let himself be carried away by his feelings, the composition was always of the greatest importance. He was also experimenting with different brush strokes, finding that long brush strokes produced different effects from bold jabs of colour. He knew he was learning a great deal with every painting. He painted what he loved and hoped other people would love the finished pictures. He drew comfort from every acre of his land, they weren't the most fertile in the area, but to him they were home and Wales. His love of his country and his countrymen was the great lesson the war had taught him.

Chapter eighteen

'Tada, can I rely on you to go on running Hendre Ddu now that I'm unable to? How do you feel about Cefn Hebog? Now that that youngster, Isaac Jenkins, is such a good manager and he soon to get married, I'm hoping that you'll be satisfied to let him bring up his little family there. When you do choose to retire, well it's your place, you know that, and I'll manage to re-house the family, building them a new house if necessary. But I'd like to know that I can depend on you for the next ten or fifteen years.'

'Of course you can. This is my family and my duty lies here. And though I say it myself, you'd find it difficult to manage without me. I'm turned fifty as you know but I reckon I'm still able to do a good day's work.'

'You needn't tell me that. I realise it every day and old Prosser tells me the same thing every time we stop to talk. The farm is beginning to do well and it's all down to you.'

'It's down to all of us, even to the women who keep us so well fed and healthy. Aye, we're a good team at the moment. And I'm not forgetting your contributions either, my lad. It's due to you that we can make really worthwhile purchases like the new tractor and can enhance our stock when we need to. Money well spent is a great blessing.'

'I've only got one major worry. I'm afraid poor May is really suffering at seeing Catrin and Lowri both so happily pregnant.'

'It's very hard for both of you. Graham, though, keeps on saying that it might still happen. You haven't been married a full two years yet and apparently some women become pregnant after ten years.'

'So I tell May, but I can see the deadness in her eyes whenever I do. She thinks our marriage is a failure. She even speaks now of going to spend a month or two with her father to shorten the winter.'

'It might be a good thing for her and for her poor father who must be very lonely without her. Perhaps she'll come back in a more positive mood. I should encourage her to go if I were you.'

The one who objected to May's journey was Mari Elen. She wanted to go with her. 'You know how I love my Grandpa. I want to stay with him for two months too.'

'Cariad, we'd all miss you too much. And you'd miss your old Dad wouldn't you?'

'I suppose so. Why can't he come to live with us here? He's May's father and he could have the little room next to mine.'

'May will ask him to come to stay in the late spring, when it's your birthday, and you can send him a letter of invitation.'

Mari Elen had to be satisfied with that.

Tom missed May and felt aggrieved that she had left him for so long. Sometimes he wished he had sinned so that she really had something to punish him for.

He longed for Maudie but he hadn't seen her since taking her the mourning clothes for her aunt's funeral and she hadn't answered his one short letter. He wondered if she had opened her little village shop and how it was getting on. He had a feeling that she would succeed in anything she set her mind to, she had a fine brain. What a dreadful injustice that she'd had to leave school at fourteen with no prospects of any work except domestic work. He felt sure that a Labour Government would improve life for working-class children, so that many of the brightest should have the opportunities of education.

Whenever Lottie had a letter from Maudie she would pass details of her new life to Lowri, but Tom could never be sure that Lowri would consider them worth passing on. Finally he decided to ask Lottie for any news she might have.

'Yes, well she opened the shop a couple of months ago and she's working hard. She has to be open before the men go to work so that they can call in for a newspaper or a packet of cigarettes and she can't close until they're all back in the evening. She makes toffee in the evening and her home-made treacle toffee is very popular. Do you remember that we used to make it here when Nano was in a good mood? It's very good for colds and coughs. But she's very worried about little Ianto, he's bored when she's in the shop because of course he doesn't have all the interests he had here, aunties and uncles and all his friends and cousins.'

'And that school teacher is still calling on her, I suppose?'

Tom, desperately trying to sound nonchalant, succeeded in making Lottie stare at him, as though understanding something for the first time. 'Harry Hughes. Yes, I think so. But she doesn't care for him, I know that much. She's told me that she never intends to get married. She's too independent, and besides she'd have to live with his mother.'

'But I thought you told us his mother was dead. Didn't he sell all her good furniture to buy his motor car?'

'But she didn't die, she just moved in with him. You see, the poor woman had a stroke last spring and needs a great deal of looking after. Maudie wouldn't get herself involved in anything like that. You'd have to love someone a lot before you'd take on a mother-in-law with a stroke. I would do it for him, yes, but he's never looked my way.'

'The man's a silly fool.'

'But that's men for you, Mister Tom. Getting someone decent to love them and look after them is not what they're after. What they want is someone beautiful like Maudie, someone like the girls in the movies, that's what men want.'

Tom sighed. 'Shall I tell her that you were asking after her?' Lottie asked slyly.

'Oh, yes. And tell her I wish her well, with all my heart.'

'With all your heart. Yes, I'll remember that bit. I'll be writing to her on Sunday and I won't forget that bit.'

One Monday morning when he hadn't heard from May for over a week, he sent another brief letter to Maudie. 'I'd love to come to see how you're getting on. No, not that, I'd just love to see you. Would it be possible?'

He had a letter by return of post. He rose abruptly from the table, putting it in his pocket until he was on his own in his room. 'It would be possible. I'd love to see you. But Lottie's let me know that May is away and thought you might be feeling lonely. I don't think anything has really altered for you. You are married, as you reminded me in your last letter. And if you came here you know – and I know – what would happen. I think it's probably better that we remain each other's secret love.'

He knew she was right. He learnt her letter by heart and then tore it into tiny fragments and burnt them feeling he was almost burning a part of himself. His father's words came back to him. 'May came here because of a whim of Nano's and you married her because she was a pleasant girl and seemed suitable.' He hadn't waited for love because he had no idea that the many-splendoured thing existed outside poetry. How was he to know that a broken heart did seem the best way to describe what had happened to him; that something inside him really did seem to be broken and bleeding?

There was a gentle knock on his door. He didn't want to speak to anyone but very unwillingly opened the door. It was Lowri. At the moment he felt she was the only one he could bear to speak to. 'What is it, Lowri?'

'That's just what I wanted to ask you. What is it Tom? You rushed off as though there was a swarm of bees after you. Have you had some bad news? Don't keep it to yourself, love. If I'm not the one you can confide in, please confide in your father. He will do everything he can to help you, I know that. Oh, and you left one of your letters on the table, here's one from May, look.'

'Thank you, Lowri. I have had some bad news, but it doesn't seem so bad now that you're here. I'll come back and you can make me another cup of tea and I'll try not to be so foolish.'

'Is it money matters, Tom?'

'I'll be honest with you, Lowri. It's not about money but about an affair of the heart that I have had to kill in the bud. Now, do you promise not to tell anyone, not even my father?'

'I do, Tom. I promise faithfully. And I'm sure you'll do right because we all trust you and look up to you. Catrin was telling me only yesterday that she wishes Graham was more like you. Graham will discuss things, she said, but he doesn't know how to chat. A woman misses that, particularly when she's pregnant.'

Tom followed her back to the breakfast room, the letter from May unopened in his hand.

'When is Catrin coming back to live here?'

'She'll be here for the last two months and we're nearly there now.'

'Which one of you is due to have your baby first?'

'We're not too sure. We both had morning sickness at roughly the same time.'

Tom gave up all thoughts of work that morning. He stayed in the breakfast room while Lottie and Lowri cleared the table and dusted and was still there at dinner time. He found Lowri's presence very comforting, like a cold hand on a hot brow.

'And how is May?' Josi asked him when he came in.

'Her father's been taken ill with bronchitis but she hopes she won't have to stay there any longer than she'd planned. She's bought a winter coat for herself and several items of baby clothes for Catrin and Lowri.'

'It must be hard for her,' Josi said, 'but her turn will come, believe me.'

'She doesn't believe it. She's given up on me. She seems quite certain that we won't have a baby and that it's her fault. Or mine.'

Chapter nineteen

May returned to Hendre Ddu at the beginning of December. Her father had had to spend some days in hospital and would be in a convalescent home over Christmas.

Tom wished he could think that she was happy to be back, but he couldn't really believe it. Occasionally he thought they seemed like two strangers and that he had to try to get to know her again. He took her to view his new paintings and she cried out, 'Oh Tom, it's too violent'. She tried to counter her first reaction, to explain that it was the change in his style that had caused her distress, but Tom was disappointed, feeling that they'd grown further and further apart since she'd been away.

'This is modern art, May,' he said. 'Think of Cezanne and Renoir.'

'I prefer the old English Masters,' she said, 'Constable and Turner. They charm without blazing at you.'

It seemed to Tom that everyone realised that his marriage was unhappy and was ready to blame him. One evening he confided these thoughts to Lowri, but she took his arm and told him that marriage needed two people's best endeavours. 'You must try to tell May how much you love her,' Lowri said. 'It's not enough to feel love, you must express it in words. Deeds without words are not enough. I can still remember the thrill I felt when your father first told me he loved me. Of course I realised he didn't love me in the same way as he'd loved Miriam, but he loved me. Me. For days, for weeks I think, I was bathed in the glow of it.'

'Lowri, you're a wonderful woman,' Tom said. 'And I hope my father realises it. I think he does.'

'How can I be happy?' May said when he spoke lovingly to her later that evening. 'I would never have married you if I'd have realised that I wasn't to have children. I wanted at least three or four. I'd been an only child and I didn't really want that, but by this time I'd feel more than happy to have only one. I'm thirty-two in February, Tom, almost seven years older than you are and a woman's fertility drops at my age. I saw a consultant about it while I was in London and I could tell that he wasn't optimistic about my chances. He could only recommend having sex in the morning when we wake up. Would you mind waiting until then, Tom?'

'Of course not. Perhaps that will prove the remedy.'

But Tom failed to sleep, convinced of his inadequacy.

Christmas came and went. Everyone was aware of May's preoccupation. She tried to pass off her unhappiness as worry about her father, but no one was convinced, especially the two women so happily pregnant. Everyone sympathised with her but her heavy mood continued.

It was soon New Year's Day with the first farm lad arriving for Calennig soon after four in the morning. He received a sovereign for his efforts, the next, a half sovereign and then half crowns and florins until the last ones came round at about seven and were only offered sixpence, a cup of tea and a piece of Christmas cake. 'You're losers my lads,' Josi told them quite kindly. 'You've probably stopped for too much Christmas fare. Glyn Hopkins who was here before four wouldn't even stop for a swig of tea. Now then, let's have a song before you go and if you sing it with gusto it may earn you another sixpence each.'

First of all, as all the others had done, they recited a piece about their efforts. 'Mi godais yn gynnar, Mi redais yn ffyrnig, I fferm Mr Ifans i mofyn calennig. Unwaith, dwywaith, tair.' After that opening came a Christmas hymn. 'Mae'r nos yn ddu a'r gwynt nid oes, Un seren sy'n y nen,' sung in harmony by the five latecomers. It was a very good effort and suitably rewarded by Josi who felt nostalgic for the time when he was a boy taking part in the New Year's Day race. And winning it too.

It was a few days after this that they heard the sickening news from Lorna Williams.

'Oh Mister Tom. She's dead, Mister Tom, our Maudie's dead.'

Tom felt a dull thud in his head as though he'd been

hit by a very heavy weight. 'Sit down, Mrs Williams and tell us what happened.' Everything seemed to be spinning round in his head.

'She was home for Christmas, stayed the night and seemed very happy. And she told Harry Hughes who called while she was here, that he wasn't to bother her again, I heard her say that and so did Ifor. But he went down to Brynyddol again the next day, Mister Tom, and out of some devilment, Hughes said, she insisted on driving his little car on her own. She'd never driven it before though he'd told her where the gears were and showed her how the brakes worked. But he should have gone with her that first time, he realises that now. Anyway, she drove the car through the village and crashed it into the wall of the Buckley Arms. And they sent for the doctor and did all they could, but she's dead, Mister Tom, our Maudie's dead. Our firstborn.'

Josi and Lowri were in the kitchen with Tom and heard the account. Josi poured them each a drop of brandy and they all sat down and let her tell her sad tale over and over again. The words seemed to be engraved in her mind because no syllable changed in its frequent re-telling. Tom felt he was seeing it all, the car veering off the road, hitting the wall of the pub and the dreadful result. And Maudie was dead, all her young beauty stopped as though by a bullet. He tried to pull himself together, but failed and went on sitting dumbly at the kitchen table. And Josi and Lowri stayed with him so that when May joined them it appeared to be a family tragedy, each one affected. May said over and over again how sorry she was.

'I didn't much like Maudie, I admit that, I thought she took liberties, was too ready to consider herself part of the family, but I'm truly sorry that she's dead. Is there anything I can do?'

'I don't think so,' Josi said at last. 'We'll have the funeral meal here, because she worked here from the time she was a young girl, just turned fourteen, so she was part of our family in a way, and you can help with that by all means. I don't think anyone can do much at the moment. For today, I should imagine that poor Ifor and Lorna Williams and their family will want to mourn in peace. Tomorrow we'll call on them to make arrangements.'

Maudie's funeral was very different from Nano's. Nano's was a celebration of a long and active working life, where she'd made herself a vital part of the life of a family and their busy, productive farm and she had died full of years and loved and respected by everyone.

Maudie's funeral was held in the same chapel but on this occasion the sad hymns were without comfort. Even the weather was bleak, the mourners huddling together. The many young people present all seemed stunned and in tears and unable to join in the singing, Maudie's younger siblings and several young cousins and friends, including Mari Elen, sniffing and sobbing. Even the older people, who usually enjoyed a funeral sermon, finding hope and comfort in it, could hardly raise their voices that day. Grief for such a young person was more than anyone seemed able to deal with.

The funeral meal, too, failed to engender much spirit and was compared to the gatherings that had been held when one of the local boys had been killed in action. Lottie failed to hide her sorrow, her eyes were red and watery however much she attacked them with her father's handkerchief. After everyone had eaten, Josi sang another slow, sad hymn to show that the occasion was over and he felt that everyone was relieved to get away.

When most people had taken their leave, Tom found himself confronted by poor Harry Hughes.

'Thank you for arranging the funeral service. I thought it was very beautiful.' For a moment the two men stood staring at each other, neither seeming able to break away. 'She was getting on very well in the little shop, too,' Harry said at last. 'She was a lovely girl.' There was a sob in his voice. Tom squeezed his hand. Poor Harry Hughes. At that moment he loved him. Perhaps he was suffering as much as he was himself.

By this time, Lottie had squeezed her handkerchief into a ball and was pushing it into her red-rimmed eyes to try to prevent herself from crying, but the tears still escaped and overflowed onto her cheeks. Dear Lottie. Tom realised that she knew all his secrets. He smiled wanly at her but she failed to respond.

'I'm sure little Ianto will be a comfort to them all,' Josi said the next day. 'Three or four of the smaller ones were building him a snowman earlier on. I hardly recognised him in his new-for-Christmas red tam-o-shanter. He looks quite a tough little lad, what is he, almost two now I should think. I'm sure he'll enjoy the rough and tumble of living in a big family.'

'And if I know anything, May will be having him over here when they're in school,' Tom said. 'You know how she adores him.'

He'd realised so much, but it was still a devastating shock when May told him, later that evening, that she'd been over to see Lorna Williams about adopting the boy. 'You would be willing, wouldn't you Tom?' she asked, her eyes bright with tears. 'I know you love him because I've seen you together so many times in the past. I know you love him and I know you realise what it would mean to me to be able to adopt him. And Mr and Mrs Williams seem quite willing. After all they still have seven children even though poor Maudie is gone and they said they wouldn't be selfish enough to stand in Ianto's way. Darling, we could give him so much. For a year now, I've been a bitter, disappointed woman and I know I haven't been at all kind to you. But now I'm so happy I feel I could light up the world. I love you Tom, because you're going to be with me in this. And I know you're going to be a wonderful father, just as Josi was to you. Oh Tom, tell me you love him already.'

Tom had listened to the flow of words, hardly able to hold anything in his head except death, the death of his loved one. But already the life force was buffeting him again. 'Yes May, I love him already and I love you too.'

It would, in time, be a sort of healing perhaps. In time.

Yes, he knew he would be a good husband and a fond father. And he knew the tears he shed that night would be accepted as suitable for the momentous occasion. To May and Tom Evans, an adopted son, Ianto.

A Small Country
by Siân James

The first novel about Hendre Ddu

Now a feature film and television series from S4C – Calon Gaeth (2007 Bafta Cymru award winner for Best Drama/Drama Serial for Television)

First published in 1979 and now part of the Seren Classics series, *A Small Country* is the story of the Evans family; farmers in Carmarthenshire. In the summer of 1914, son Tom returns from Oxford to find the family falling apart. His handsome father has gone to live with schoolmistress Miriam Lewis, who is to have his child. His mother, broken-hearted, lies ill in bed, while his beautiful sister Catrin longs to leave for London and art college. Soon Tom's college friend Edward will arrive to holiday with them, half-aware of his attraction to Catrin but already engaged to Rose, a supporter of the Suffragettes. And Tom himself is in debt and disillusioned with his proposed legal career. He would like to manage Hendre Ddu, the family farm, but finds that family troubles and the approach of war set him on a very different course.

Sian James interweaves the lives of her characters with skill and understanding as they face the complications of family breakdown, love, war and propriety. Her ear for dialogue and eye for detail make *A Small Country* a hugely enjoyable novel.

Simply told, a moving story deeply and imaginatively embedded in its Welsh background and Welsh ways.'

– Birmingham Post